BEFORE EARTH CAME launches a new series collecting the early pioneering pulp magazine novelettes of John Russell Fearn, with the first-ever reprinting of "Before Earth Came" and "Subconscious."

Both stories abound with unbridled imagination and a sense of wonder, examples of the pioneering stories being written in SF more than 80 years ago.

In "Before Earth Came" Fearn's storyline of how alien scientists, facing the imminent utter destruction of their planet, seek to preserve their heritage by sending it to Earth, was later copied by the creators of *Superman*.

And "Subconscious" was one of the *very first* SF stories to utilize the theory of Charles Fort that "We are Property!"...a theme that has echoed down science fiction ever since!

THE GOLDEN AMAZON SAGA,
by John Russell Fearn

1. *World Beneath Ice*
2. *Lord of Atlantis*
3. *Triangle of Power*
4. *The Amethyst City*
5. *Daughter of the Amazon*
6. *Quorne Returns*
7. *The Central Intelligence*
8. *The Cosmic Crusaders*
9. *Parasite Planet*
10. *World Out of Step*
11. *The Shadow People*
12. *Kingpin Planet*
13. *World in Reverse*
14. *Dwellers in Darkness*
15. *World in Duplicate*
16. *Lords of Creation*
17. *Duel with Colossus*
18. *Standstill Planet*
19. *Ghost World*
20. *Earth Divided*
21. *Chameleon Planet* (with Philip Harbottle)

BEFORE EARTH CAME

JOHN RUSSELL FEARN

Edited by Philip Harbottle

WILDSIDE PRESS

Published by Wildside Press, LLC.
www.wildsidepress.com

CONTENTS

INTRODUCTION

BY PHILIP HARBOTTLE

Ever since January 1930 there had existed an American pulp SF adventure magazine called *Astounding Stories*, published by the Clayton group. But in the Great Depression which reached an all-time low in 1933, Clayton failed and the magazine folded. Another publisher, Street and Smith purchased the title and gave it a new lease of life under one of their top editors, F. Orlin Tremaine.

Tremaine was the stimulant the SF field needed, and he innovated a scheme for stories with daringly new and original ideas. They became termed "thought-variants." Here was an open-ended challenge for authors to pull SF out from the rut into which it was drifting. All the most capable authors took up the gauntlet, writers like Donald Wandrei, Nat Schachner, Jack Williamson, Murray Leinster—and not least English writer John Russell Fearn.

Of this group of stories—which appeared mainly in the years 1934-37—several have passed into legend, particularly Leinster's "Sidewise In Time," and Williamson's "Born of the Sun" (both 1934). Equally legendary, and audacious were Fearn's two 1936 novelettes "Mathematica" and its sequel, "Mathematica *P*lus." They were later expanded as a UK novel, *To The Ultimate* (currently scheduled to appear as an ebook).

In these stories Fearn attempted to explain the whole of creation in a mystical mathematical framework. His basic contention was that God, the Creator of the universe, is a Supreme Mathematician. His purpose is the creation of mathematics, which are actually thoughts. Out of those mathematics He creates worlds and life, and the object of His ageless existence is to strive towards the ultimate cancellation of all figures, to destroy what he has created. Only by that method can He release Himself from an eternity of mental and physical toil! Both of the original stories are currently available from Wildside in my collection *The Best of John Russell Fearn* (volume 1), along with two other of his thought-variant stories, "The Man Who Stopped the Dust" (1934) and "Deserted Universe" (1936). A further thought-variant novelette is the title story of another more recent Wildside Fearn collection, *Dynasty of the Small.*

But Fearn wrote other interesting thought-variant stories that have so far not been reprinted, and, writing in the famous US fanzine *Fantasy Magazine* in 1935, Fearn recalled how he had created these early stories:

> Then came the glorious day when *Astounding Stories* was revived and the idea of "thought-variant" stories was brought forward. Stories being vitally different, filled to the brim with new and tremendous ideas. Here at last was my outlet. I set out, with commendable assurance perhaps, to write nothing but thought-variants—and succeeded every time save one.
>
> My first effort in this direction was "The Man Who Stopped the Dust," which proved an absolute winner. The second one "The Brain of Light" received high praise but I was accused of forsaking science for sheer imagination. I admit that was correct, but just the same I got away with it. Later, I got the idea of a man never

sleeping and what might happen if this same man explored a dream. The result was "He Never Slept," published in May *Astounding Stories* for 1934. Then I wrote perhaps what I privately class as the best yarn I ever did and which later became the second best story of 1934 in science fiction[1]. "Before Earth Came" was its title, in which I disproved all theories concerning the creation of our Solar System. Sure, I got a deluge of criticism, so much so that I argued with the Editor and almost pushed out of the paper altogether. Not that that worried me. I had a grand idea and I wrote it down, and I don't suppose, even if I live to be 90 that such an idea will ever come to me again. To which some readers will probably say "Thank goodness!"

After the furore of "Before Earth Came"—which Universal films are considering for filming—I wrote a story of the subconscious mind, depicting how it was quite possible for the minds of two people of Mars to control the entire destiny of earthly people, and every bit of it was scientifically accurate. It sold like a hot cake to *Amazing Stories* in America, but so far has not had publication.[2]

Fearn's *Fantasy* article went on to detail his further stories written through 1935, and I will be quoting further from this in future collections. His article concluded:

My ideas? I don't pretend to know where I get them. Agents and editors tell me I *must* tone down a bit, and I solemnly agree—for a while. Then another great idea pops up and, either by the audacity of my imagination, else out of pity for the nutty Englishman, the Editor accepts it and again the front cover is allotted to me…

1   As voted in *Fantasy Magazine*.
2   "Subconscious" was eventually published in *Amazing* in its August 1936 issue.

Science fiction is an art, I agree—but it affords to any writer with imagination a terrific wealth of ideas. England is missing a tremendous and vital factor in its modern literature. I do not suggest that we should emulate the almost sensational work of the Americans— we should tone down to truly British dignity, but even then science is superb and vitally interesting to the most uninterested person when written by a master hand. Who in England ever heard of Jack Williamson, John Taine, John W. Campbell, etc.? Nobody! Yet in America they are the greatest of SF writers breathing. It is said by a certain prominent SF editor that if an author can write SF he can write anything. I agree with him, but all the same an ordinary author cannot write science fiction. It is an art—and a science. As to the future, for myself I shall go on writing very scientific and very unscientific stories. Whatever happens I must use my imagination. It was given me as a gift, I presume, and nothing consummates the perfection of a gift as usage."

In this first volume of a new series of collections, I am presenting the first-ever reprinting of "Before Earth Came" and "Subconscious."

I believe that they will interest modern readers who are prepared to suspend their disbelief of the (often deliberate) scientific infelicities, in order to enjoy their unbridled imagination and sense of wonder, and to accept these pioneering stories as fascinating examples of what was being written in SF more than 80 years ago. And they will find that they were often influential as to what came later. Here are just two examples:

In "Before Earth Came" Fearn's storyline of how alien scientists, facing the imminent utter destruction of their planet, seek to preserve their heritage by sending it to

Earth, was later copied by the creators of *Superman*—for Jir read Krypton!

And "Subconscious" was one of the *very first* SF stories to utilize the theory of Charles Fort that "We are Property!"…a theme that has echoed down science fiction ever since!

BEFORE EARTH CAME

I.

The winding path across the moor took the young man and woman in a wide detour, bringing them at length, when the warm spring evening had settled upon the countryside, to a little knoll overlooking the lights of the village in which they lived.

Quietly, as though with some subconscious union of thought, they seated themselves on the newborn grass and gazed down into the uncertainty of lights and shadows where lay their homes; then gradually they looked upward to the west, with its orange and vermilion flushes, and at last toward the purple gulf of deepening night—night blazoned with the splendor of rapidly appearing stars,

"It's—it's all very wonderful, yet very strange," the girl whispered, her chin tilted in the air. "I don't know why, but tonight the stars and the quiet frighten me a little. I mean, to think of your mind being sent backward into time. Lee, it makes me afraid!"

Lee Carnforth took her hand reassuringly. Bred of the village though he was, there was upon him the indelible impress of nobility, inherited from some long dead and forgotten ancestor. The fire of command kindled in the blue eyes; the powerful, well-developed figure and magnificent head were something curiously alien to his parents—both simple, village souls.

"Mary," he said softly, tightening his grip upon her hand, "you mustn't worry about me. I'd trust your father to the end of time. He's an extraordinary man—in some ways the most brilliant in the scientific world. So why on earth shouldn't I accede to his request? After all, I can't get his permission to marry you by any other means!"

"I know that, but—" The girl stopped, her gray eyes troubled. For a space her delicate profile was outlined against the light of the moon-rise.

"It's the unknown that worries and appalls me," she explained at last. "Up there in space is nothing but mystery; time is an even bigger mystery. You and I are just ordinary people, denizens of a planet which we call Earth. Why should father want to unlock the doors of the unknown—probe backward through time? Beyond the beyond! Lee, my dear, I am afraid—for you."

"Mary, that is no way to encourage your young man to undertake a hazardous feat," remarked a crisp and practical voice, at which the two looked up, startled, and scrambled to their feet.

Dr. Ainsworth, Mary's father, was standing only a few feet away, wearing, as ever, his faded soft hat and thick, fur-collared overcoat. Smoke rose on the windless air from his meerschaum pipe.

"Why, father, I never knew—"

"All right—all right. I take walks sometimes, you know. Tonight is so peaceful, so still, that I—"

The girl moved forward and took her father's arm; her face was intent and serious.

"Father, won't you please release Lee from his promise? Please say you will! This is his last night, you know."

"You speak as though I'm going to execute Lee, or something! Nothing of the sort! Your plea, Mary, is sponsored by ignorance. There is no danger!"

"Oh, I know you think nothing of scientific experiments. To you, they're all harmless. But unlocking the past—"

"Poetic, but a trifle erroneous. Here, sit down, and I'll explain to you both the nature of the idea at the back of the experiment,"

The two young people obeyed and listened intently, though Lee's eyes were fixed on Mary's reddish-gold hair in the moonlight and her earnest, classical face. For a moment an odd idea that he'd seen her seated in a similar way in similar circumstances somewhere in the past occurred to him; then he decided it was pure fancy.

"All our knowledge," the doctor began slowly, "is purely inherited and stamped on our brain cells, so to speak; the remoter knowledge is so buried beneath the accumulation of new impressions that it fails to affect us at all. We concentrate only on the present, with flashes from the past at times when something occurs to bring back a memory, or excitation of the particular cell storing that memory. We say a man loses his memory; actually his brain cells are out of alignment and he is existing in a condition that he—or else his parent who handed down the impression—also once lived in.

"The parent always hands down all knowledge to the child—except in the case of the mental defective—but the child has no idea of this fact unless the new cells are deadened so as to permit the remoter impressions to have sway. That is what we call hereditary traits, where some particularly forceful series of impressions from the parent are handed down to the child, so vividly as to be vital above the new impressions the child has gained.

"Now, I have an electric energy of the same type as that in the human body itself, and through years of experiment I have made a ray of this electric energy, narrow enough, of needle-pointed thinness, to touch only one cell in a brain, and leave the remainder free. This ray is capable of deadening, for a given period, brain cells—layer by layer—until the deepest set of cells is reached, which of course contain the oldest impressions—those of the primordial, I presume.

"Also, I have equipped my laboratory, as you know, Mary, with a machine which is magnetic in principle and absorbs the impressions from one single brain cell. These brain-cell impressions, in the first place, were begotten by waves of light and radiations of sound, seen and heard by some remote ancestor. My converter transforms these cell impressions into the original light and sound, and the impressions are thrown on a zinc-sulphide screen—much the same as X-ray impressions.

"Experiments on the brain cells of dogs have revealed the dog down to its first appearance on Earth. Then, removal of my cell-deadening ray, a rapid restorative, and the subject is normal again, with no remembrance of the past. During the test, I presume, the person must actually seem to live the particular incident over again. So now you know why I want a human subject to travel backward, yet never actually move."

"But, father, what good will it do?" Mary demanded. "What use will it be to the world to know what's been in the past? It's written down in history—"

"Yes; but we've had to take the writer's word for it," the doctor replied calmly. "There is much we may find—or, rather, that Lee will find for us. I would go my-self without hesitation, but there is nobody to operate the machinery. You understand, my boy?" He glanced at Lee.

"I understand," the young giant assented quietly.

"Somewhere in the past you have belonged to people of high birth," the scientist went on thoughtfully. "So has my dear Mary. I have nothing classical or regal about me neither had her dear mother—yet both of you, possessing as you do quite average-looking parents, are obviously begotten of some high, aristocratic stock. By tracing backward, Lee, we shall ultimately arrive at your ances-tors and find out where you came from."

"Couldn't—couldn't I go with him, father?" the girl asked suddenly.

"No, my dear. I have only one ray, and it takes a person of great physical power to last through the ex-periment. I'm afraid I might lose you—you are a woman, and weaker. Which reminds me—I am totally unable to understand why women are weaker physically than men! My experiment may even clear that up."

"I think we'd better be moving," Lee remarked. "It's getting cool here."

"Indeed it is, my boy. Yes; come along."

* * * *

At eight o'clock the following morning, Lee arrived at the doctor's home—an almost monastic place sepa-rated from the main bulk of the village. He found the elderly scientist and Mary in the laboratory at the rear of the residence, after a frozen-faced manservant had ad-mitted him.

"Splendid!" the doctor exclaimed, advancing and shaking the young man by the hand. "Right on time! You see, I prefer early morning for the experiment because the brain is fresh and active after repose—toward night there is too much poison in the blood. I don't think you've seen my apparatus before, have you? Here is the experimental table on which you will lie; above is the ray machine. Over there is the screen for recording the impressions—which, by the way, I have decided to photograph."

"Photograph?" Lee repeated.

"Yes! I have there a professional talking-picture camera and microphone. As the sound and vision occasioned by the brain cells appear on the screen there, I shall make a talking film of them, so that there will be an everlasting record of your adventure. You see, when you recover, you will remember nothing of your experiences, and naturally you will want to know what happened."

"I see." Lee nodded. "Of course, when I come back to normal, past impressions will be once more buried."

The doctor said that was true and turned to busy himself with his apparatus.

Quietly Mary stole forward and gripped the young man's hand. "Lee, I'm still afraid! It's all so horribly inhuman—"

Lee smiled. "Don't worry, Mary—I trust your father. And—"

"Now we're ready!" the doctor's voice intervened fussily. "Mary, please don't delay us. Now, Lee, lie on the table, if you please."

With a firm clasp of the girl's hand, Lee obeyed, stretching his lissom body on the glittering metal of the experimental table. The doctor's semi-bald head and round face popped up beside him. "All right? That's excellent! Now—"

There followed a clicking of switches from the control board and the soft, beating pulsation of a generator. On the far wall a safety valve glowed pink. The doctor drew across the window curtains, plunging the laboratory into half-darkness.

"Everything is set," he remarked. "Merely lie down and compose yourself. That's fine. Now—go!"

He snapped in the master switch amid a flaring of blue sparks.

Almost instantly, Lee's body relaxed, and his respiration dropped to an amazing shallowness. The color slowly ebbed from his cheeks.

"Father! What—" Mary began helplessly, digging her nails into her palms with the intensity of the moment.

"Nothing's wrong!" the scientist said. "Simply incipient rigor mortis; that's all. Won't develop any further. In a sense, Lee is dead, yet alive. Now for the ray—but first we'll want the Z beam."

"Z beam? What's that?"

"I forgot to mention it to you last night." The doctor fiddled among his labyrinth of switches and presently connected up a small, single-lensed projector. A pale-cream beam shot forth and enveloped the young man's head. But most remarkable of all was the fact that his face seemed actually to vanish. Instead there was a perfect view of his skull with the distinct convolutions of the brain within.

"Father, it's horrible!" the girl gasped.

Quite oblivious to her cry, the scientist murmured: "My Z beam is indeed a masterpiece! You see, Mary, it is based on the principle of Rontgen's X-rays, only that instead of using barium platinocyanide or hydrated potassium platinocyanide screens, as is used for X rays, this beam causes instant transparency, without the necessity for a screen on which to project the image.

"The Z beam is of a different wave length to anything known to ordinary science, and apparently causes all external tissues to vanish, but leaves internal tissue quite visible. In a sense, the Z beam stops light radiation from external flesh, leaving the interior bared, as it were. I have to do this to determine which cells have to be deadened. Now for the next stage."

Breathing rapidly, the doctor switched on yet another device and stared with burning eyes at a flickering needle within an air-exhausted case. The depressing of various buttons caused the needle to switch around to various numbers, a performance which Mary watched with *a* gradual widening of her eyes.

"What—what is it all?" she stammered at last. "Electricity?"

"No—no! Each brain cell emits a certain frequency, you understand; during my experiments I've tabulated the frequencies that relate to certain impressions. Inside this meter is an invisible recoiling wave length, which, when tuned on a brain, shows on the meter which cell is being affected. Then I know which cells to deaden. Don't stand there, girl—you are between the vibration and Lee's brain. See, the needle has dropped to zero through the intervention of your body. Get out of my way!"

Unwittingly curt in his excitement, the scientist hastily computed figures from the dial and then switched on his cell-deadening ray. A brilliant pencil of fire, as it appeared, almost so thin as to be two-dimensional, stabbed from the apparatus slung over the experimental table, and, with a pair of heavily insulated guiders, the doctor directed the beam until its needle point was focused upon Lee's plainly visible brain. Manifestly, the force must have passed through the almost-invisible skull bone and into the cells below. Lee made no movement, but lay as one dead.

Still in silence the doctor worked.

"So far, so good!" he exclaimed at last, the ray evidently in position to his liking. "Now, let us see what the screen has to show."

He turned aside to his instruments, and presently there came another type of buzzing sound as the vibration screen was switched on. For a space nothing intelligible was apparent—only a cloudy nebulous mystery. Intently the two watched.

"Look! *Look!*" the doctor insisted at last, gripping his daughter's arm.

She gazed at the screen with widening eyes, astounded at the sight she beheld.

"It's succeeded!" her father exulted. "The camera, quick!"

With quick strides he crossed to it and livened up the microphone. Almost at the same moment the sound system connected to the brain-vibration screen began to function, and sound accompanied the astonishing, clear-cut pictures projected thereon.

II.

Lee Carnforth, the instant the doctor had closed the master switch of his apparatus, relapsed apparently into a world of complete darkness—an incredible world in which he was apparently a disembodied spirit. In a sense he was alive, and yet dead. He realized he was not breathing; that his heart was apparently still, and yet he was able to see—hazily.

For a space he lay gazing into a gulf. There came a strange sensation of fleeting pain—the doctor's probing ray—then speed, irresistible speed that seemed to buoy him upward and hurl him helplessly into the cosmos.

Lee tried to shut out the vision of coldly glittering stars and failed. He was in an abyss, in which he saw nought but stars, millions of stars, rushing and surging tumultuously, without organized precision or orbital law. Frozen terror was within him; a sense of overwhelming helplessness. Soundless onrush through infinity—an infinity which somewhere, he realized, was nought but time.

Abruptly the onrush ceased, and he became momentarily still, then he shot forth again. His memories became clearer and clearer as the ray continued. Through the frightful reaches of forgotten time his ideas hurtled—backward and ever backward, through the knowledge of his ancestors, even past them, and still backward. Already he had exceeded by far the limit anticipated by the doctor, was indeed now in a period before Earth itself had come.

Still the void swirled and changed, moved and gyrated. Star clusters rose up, evanescent, to vanish in infinity. A comet flashed and was gone. Stars shot through amazing magnitudes of brightness. The whole pattern of the eternal lay spread before him—a gigantic, complex enigma.

Then the sickening sense of speed began to diminish, and with it his powers of understanding began to lose their clarity also. He found himself watching the stars with a bemused sensation, unable to understand or comprehend them. Strange lusts and primitive passions were within him; an extraordinary desire to kill and destroy. There came a fleeting conviction of superhuman strength, then incredible weakness. Even more his power of reasoning weakened, until at last he was in a blackness devoid even of stars.

How long this peculiar condition lasted he had no knowledge, but ultimately there appeared on the ray-less obscurity a tiny streak of gray, widening rapidly, until presently he beheld, for the first time, evidences of life—strange, complex evidences that mystified him, shooting as they did in snapshotting confusion before him.

A vision of an unknown laboratory rose up and was gone; another one appeared. He was staggering along some rocky defile with a limp woman in his arms. The air seemed smoky. Another picture of a blazing star shot across the view—and was gone. Darkness swirled across and blotted out an enigmatical scene of a young and lovely woman who looked oddly like Mary, seated on a mighty fallen boulder, while at the back of her loomed the mass of a colossal city of white stone. Strange, incomprehensible scenes! The black deepened. All sense of remembrance left him, but with it came a conviction that he could move.

The uncertainty of things passed. His gaze alighted upon a massive, intellectual face, heavily bearded, bending over him. Bright lights were trained upon his recumbent form; he was lying upon a surgical bed of some type or other, with a solitary surgeon surveying him.

Slowly, vaguely puzzled, he rose up, then glanced down at the semi-Grecian robe he was wearing—a sleeveless raiment with a golden girdle around the waist. His hair was curiously long.

"What—what's the matter?" he asked at last.

There remained in his brain no remembrance of his travel through time. This fact alone rendered him incapable of surprise that he was speaking in a strange language. To him, it seemed the correct language, for he had no knowledge of any other. At the reply from the surgeon, he listened intently.

"Obviously, my son, you are exceedingly vigorous this morning. I've tried to anaesthetize you, so that I may conduct the brain test, but you are too strong to go under. No matter—it cannot be helped. But what causes this strength? Why did you so easily overcome the anaesthetic? Why?" The surgeon's eyes were puzzled.

Lee considered for a moment. Strange thoughts were suddenly in the back of his mind; unformed, scarcely definable, thoughts. A conviction of some other life, light-centuries from his present state. Then he shrugged his broad shoulders, slid off the table, and drew a robe of purple and gold about him.

"You can conduct the brain experiment later, Laznor," he said curtly. "But first tell me the exact reason why you want my brain? You have explained that only to my august father—not to me. I have a right to know."

"Truly," Laznor conceded. After a pause he began slowly: "You know that we plan the greatest feat of science ever attempted in the history of Jir?"

Lee nodded.

The fogs of the anaesthetic had now cleared; he was, of course, the son of Varnos, Lord of Jir, Jir being the planet itself—a synthetic planet with an artificial luminary for a sun. His name was Morna, and had he not, the day before, offered his brain for the cause of Jirian science?

"Our greatest feat," continued the surgeon, "will be the creation of an actual solar system and providing that system with life akin to ours."

Morna remembered. "Yes; I recollect your plans now," he said. "But I would really prefer to know something more first. There is much that I must see and do. I must visit Hanzan, the astronomer and chemist, since he is the prime mover in this experiment."

"So be it," the master surgeon assented gravely. "I await your pleasure, my son."

Morna nodded and left the operating theater, presently reaching the exterior of the great building. The City of Science lay stretched before him—a familiar scene that occasioned him no wonder. Monstrous edifices of blue-white stone gleamed in the light of the artificial sun—white, spotless streets. The quiet, thoughtful figures of men and women came and went. All was quite familiar—a typical day.

Morna stepped down into the main street and, nodding to those whom he recognized, made his way to the domain of Hanzan, the chief astronomer and chemist. He entered the expert's observatory not ten minutes afterward.

"Greetings, Morna!" the astronomer said solemnly, bowing. "This is an honor you confer upon me. I thought you were to undergo a preliminary experiment this morning?"

"I was, but I desire to understand more fully the nature of this gigantic test of your science. What precisely are you going to do?"

"Create a solar system, my son."

"I know. But—is it really necessary?"

The astronomer hesitated, doubt in his eyes. Slowly he inclined his white head.

"Yes; it is very necessary. Our knowledge must be passed on to another race, and that race, growing up through the scale of evolution, will eventually come to possess our learning. So our greatness will again flourish, even though it be millions of years in the future."

"You speak as though we're destined to be destroyed!"

Hanzan said gravely: "Our world can last only a few days longer, my son. We are a doomed race."

"A doomed race! But—"

"You are aware that Jir has recently been subjected to terrific earthquakes, landslides, tempests and—"

"Yes! But I thought that they were natural happenings," Morna protested. "Today is so peaceful!"

"Yes, today is indeed quiet—a blessed respite. But the hour of our doom is very near; that is why we must not delay the brain experiment that Laznor is to perform upon you. We have much to do and little time to do it in. You see, my tests of these surface disturbances have led me to discover that our planet is subject to that which a natural planet is not—namely an explosive cancer. You see, this globe was first generated from gas, when we populated an almost freezing world far out in the cosmos, and we fashioned what we considered a perfect world for our work and migrated to it—here. For two thousand years all has gone well, but now we find that the gas, from which we kindled our planet is atomic in nature and, being so, constantly spreading.

"In the early years of this synthetic planet's life the gas was dormant, for the surface was young and pliable, and the gas could escape through numberless interstices into the open. Now that the planet has become older and the crust has solidified, it results in the imprisoned gas being unable to escape, and all the time it is growing. This results in inevitable compression and resultant expansion. The gas blows itself out and causes earthquakes and landslides. Terrific though these disasters are, they only release a tiny fragment of the actual gas mass within the core. The rate of expansion is far ahead of that of liberation. So, my experiments have shown, our world will be burst asunder by the ever-increasing pressure, before many days have passed."

"Why wasn't I told of this before?" Morna demanded, appalled.

"I found it out myself only when it was too late," Hanzan answered in a troubled voice. "You would have been told in good time. I told only your father, and he refrained from informing the populace in case it might cause panic, despite the sanely balanced knowledge and characteristic fatalism of our race. There is no escape, my son."

"Surely a bore can be made to let the gas escape—"

Hanzan smiled faintly. "You know as well as I do this planet is solid rock—not soil, as are many natural worlds. Even with the materials at our command, it would take four years to sink a bore to the correct depth to be serviceable, and we have only as many days. Space-travel we could adopt, of course, since we have frequently crossed the void, but there would be difficulty in finding a planet suitable for us. Therefore your father has willed that our race end; or at least we of Jir shall cease to be. Destiny has decided that our course is finished. This being so, we shall pass on all our knowledge to another race, as yet unborn, and you, if you will consent, will escape death by that very reason."

Morna seated himself and looked at the expert in vague surprise. "I didn't know all this, Hanzan," he remarked. "How can I hand down our knowledge and escape death thereby?"

"I will tell you. What we propose is this: When the artificial solar system has been completed and is satisfactorily installed in space, we shall hurl to the planet most likely to sustain life of our type a mass of protoplasm—synthetically made, of course. This protoplasm will differ from normal protoplasm in two things. There will be a male and a female protoplasm, capable of co-union as time passes, by chemical affinity, and secondly both will be impregnated with the cells of a male and female brain respectively, which, according to Laznor's calculations, will ultimately result in two independent sexes, such as we are, possessing male and female characteristics.

"Hence the experiment on your brain, to see if it is the type we need. Then, if all is satisfactory, the main cells of your brain—about which Laznor will tell you more when the time comes—will be placed in the artificial male protoplasm. Subsequently you and the female protoplasm will start to grow on the new world; the inevitable law of evolution will result in the rudimentary type of two-legged animal—then the ape, then the savage man, and finally civilized man; so a civilization as powerful as ours will ultimately rise up. Why? Because our knowledge will be condensed into two brains before we die. Evolution will bring it forth."

"Do you expect me to live millions of years, then?" Morna inquired dazedly.

"Of course not! You will die, but not before you have begotten others, who will possess your knowledge also. They will do likewise, and so the evolution will go on, until— Well, who knows? In the unthinkable future you may again be living, in some other form. Perhaps similar to what you are now."

"And this new planet? Suppose it blows up as this one is going to do?"

Hanzan smiled grimly. "This time there will be no such mistake. We have guarded against it."

"Are you quite sure life will live on the synthetic planet you are going to single out?"

"There is no reason to doubt it. Solar cosmic rays reacting upon our protoplasm will be bound—according to the experiments we've made—to form the correct chemical reagent, construed as life itself."

Morna considered. At last he smiled and shrugged. "I might just as well die being of benefit to the race as not. What are you going to call this solar system? The names of the different planets, I mean?"

"It all depends upon how many planets we succeed in wresting from the mighty flaming gas which we shall kindle in the void," Hanzan replied. "The task of finding names is simple enough. Do you understand now what is before us? The need for urgency?"

"Yes. Thank you for the explanations. I shall be able to watch this solar system created, I suppose?

"Most certainly! Here in the laboratory, at sundown tomorrow. I am preparing the apparatus even now. When the time comes it will be fully explained to you. And now may I prevail upon you to return to Laznor that he may make his brain test?"

Morna nodded. "Yes; now that I realize the necessity for speed, I'll go immediately."

* * * *

Somewhat to his surprise, Morna found that the brain test of the master surgeon of Jir did not occupy a great deal of time. He was obviously satisfied with his experiment, and when his complicated task was over he stood absently contemplating a scroll of thin metal upon which he had engraved, with a peculiar vibratory instrument, a mass of symbols and numerals, computations born of the amazingly advanced science of Jir.

"A fine brain indeed!" he murmured, as Morna glanced at him and then slid from the experimental table. "With those brain cells removed, Morna, and embodied in the male protoplasm, we can create what ultimately will prove a master race." He paused, then a shadow crossed his learned face. "My son, I am troubled," he admitted quietly. "Deeply troubled indeed."

"Why? What's the matter?"

"I am wondering what brain to use for the female protoplasm. Perhaps you can help me?"

"I know of nobody, Laznor."

"Not even the Princess Axata?" the master surgeon inquired gently.

Morna's eyes flamed. Fiercely he seized Laznor's shoulder. "Axata is not for experiment; she is my betrothed! The only daughter of the second Lord of Jir, one degree lower in social scale than I, and you dare to suggest that she, with her beauty and—"

"I am not concerned with her beauty; only her brain," Laznor answered calmly. "Can you not see that I am trying to spare you unpleasant tidings, my son? The Princess Axata is the only woman in all Jir who will answer our purpose, and what science claims, it must have. That you two are betrothed, that you love each other, means nothing. In Jir, there is only science. Of course, if you can persuade her in your own way, it will make the task simpler."

"You command me to do it?" Morna asked with sudden quietness,

"Perhaps," Laznor admitted with a shrug. "In any case, she will be taken; better that you try it voluntarily than learn the news afterward, In any event, you have only a few days to live; why, therefore, do you worry?"

"It's not that; it's just that I cannot tolerate the thought of Axata being sacrificed on the altar of our science. It is brutal—cold!"

"In a way, I understand your emotions," Laznor answered quietly, taking the young man's shoulder. "But listen to the counsel of a man who has lived three thousand or more years. We are a scientific race; all our principles and motives are founded upon it. Defy science you cannot, even if you be the ruler himself. Science has chosen two beings out of the people of Jir to perpetuate our race—the Princess Axata and yourself. You can do nothing but submit. So if you try to persuade her yourself, you may feel happier about it; either way, she will obey our behest.

"Our protoplasm, the female one, must contain impregnations of female brain. It is our plan to make our future race of a slightly different caliber to ourselves. We of Jir are either entirely masculine or entirely feminine. The perpetuators of our race will not be so. In some cases, as the evolution proceeds, there will be distinct traces of the man in women, and women in the men. We have learned that rigid male and female is not an ideal combination; each should have something of the other to make the perfect union. You understand?"

"I think so." Morna nodded, calm now. "Very well, Laznor; I will suggest your plan to Axata. I am seeing her at sundown."

"Excellent. If you succeed in persuading her, you will feel less unhappy about the matter. You have; much to pay for being highborn, my son—throughout our history it has always been the rulers that have made the sacrifices; the masses escape. Oh, and before you go, please remember that the brain test has left your brain now in a highly impressionable and malleable state; that is to say it will take and retain all the impressions you receive from now on until the final impregnation in the male protoplasm. So have a care what you do and think about, as your experiences may affect the whole destiny of a race as yet unborn. Struggle to preserve the calmness, nobility, and lack of evil motives for which Jir is famed."

"Very well, Laznor. Nothing will upset me, I promise you."

III.

The mighty bulk of the City of Science was etched out in blackest silhouette against the flaming crimson of sunset when Morna met the Princess Axata. She came, as ever, with a light but dignified tread, following the short, broad road from the city itself, until she reached the little knoll where Morna was sitting, chin cupped on hand, staring down into the spreading ramifications of the city below him. Slowly, almost imperceptibly, the basin below was filling with darkness; here and there spots of light sprang into being as radium lights were switched on.

"Thinking, Morna?" Axata asked gently, and at the sound of her voice he jumped up and seized her two hands. Seriously he looked into her perfect face—smooth, classical, determined. She gently withdrew her hands as her gray eyes studied his troubled expression.

"What can it be that troubles the son of the Lord of Jir?" she asked presently, half smiling.

"Axata—there is something vitally important which I must tell you."

For a while the two sat in silence. At last Morna turned to her.

"Axata, tonight, somehow, my mind feels as if it had experienced this same action before, as if you and I have sat together on a knoll overlooking a valley—somewhere. Oddly enough, it is not so much that we have done.it, but that we *shall* do it—somewhere in the far distant future."

"How strangely you are talking, Morna! Was that what you wanted to tell me?"

"No—not that." Morna's strong face set for a moment, then again he took hold of the girl's hand. Quietly he told her the story of Hanzan and Laznor, and when he had concluded he relapsed into moody silence, leaving the girl gazing pensively heavenward.

"I can hardly believe it," she said at last. "That our planet is doomed! It is almost unthinkable! And you and I are to give our brains, our very lives, in order that we may be the promoters of a new race on a world yet unmade. It—it is all so incredible!"

"I know. It's inhuman, in fact," Morna growled.

"For you, at least." she answered quietly. "It is an honor to serve our planet, and as we are the highest born, it is our bounden duty. I shall willingly give my brain—"

She paused and smiled whimsically. "After all, why not? A few days more, and then—" She stopped and shrugged, her shoulders expressively.

"I know that, Axata, but we love each other—"

"Yes; and in that we are something of a phenomenon," she answered. "All marriages as a rule are predetermined and predestined—especially among us of the higher circle. Eugenics determine the number of children; we have examinations of fitness. There's not much love left after all that, as a rule. With us, it is somehow quite different. We have been chosen by the higher circle as mates, and by a curious coincidence we happen to love each other dearly as well. Perhaps that is why we are to be parted."

"I can't stand the thought of your having to undergo the experiment," Morna muttered.

The girl gently took his arm. "There is one thing you seem to forget, Morna. In any ease, we shall have to part, so isn't it better that we part in the same way? Don't forget, as we pass through the eternities of time and space, we may ultimately come together again. It is possible. On the new planet, when we evolve finally into a civilized state, we may meet again. If we do, surely no barrier can rise up to prevent our recognizing each other?"

Morna shook his head. "In that time the primary cells that started the business will have undergone widely diversified types. Still, it's no use defying the edict of our masters. We have to do as we're told."

"Exactly—so why worry?" Axata seemed curiously philosophical. "Between us we will start a race in which men are men and entirely without fear or evil motives; and women are likewise entirely unafraid, and every whit as strong as the men. Nothing can stop that happening. I don't altogether approve of Laznor's idea to incorporate something of a man in a woman, and vice versa; surely it is better that we remain as we are—entirely man or entirely woman?"

Morna shrugged. "I suppose he has it all weighed up. Perhaps he's right. Tomorrow you must visit Laznor and undergo a brain test; he'll also do something that will make your brain malleable to impressions, just as he has mine. So be careful, as I am, that nothing happens that may impress you so much as to hand on the belief to the future women."

The girl smiled faintly. "Yes—that would be strange," she admitted slowly, and sat for a long interval pondering on the infinite complexities of time and space.

* * * *

The following day, the brain-operation test upon the Princess Axata having been pronounced satisfactory by the master surgeon, the two made their way to the abode of Hanzan, upon whose apparently aged shoulders rested the incumbency of creating an entire solar system. When the two entered he was standing in deep thought in the midst of a multitude of apparatus, but he was quick to give them the Jirian salutation of highest respect.

"Greetings, Princess—and you, Morna! What brings you here?"

"Since we are so involved in the future of the synthetic solar system, we thought you might be able to give us an explanation as to how this system will be created," Morna replied, a trifle tentatively under the ancient's keen eyes.

The astronomer considered for a moment, then he smiled pleasantly.

"Be seated," he said gravely, and when the two had complied he paced slowly up and down before them.

"It will take all the scientific resources of Jir to complete this final master experiment," he said at last, pausing. "By streams of vibration projected into a chosen spot in space—approximately four hundred millions of miles distant in the void, where there is at present a phenomenal lack of stars and galaxies—we shall kindle out of the utter zero of space a flaming mass of fire, which is to be the sun of the future solar system."

"How?" Morna ventured. "Cold can't create heat, surely?"

"Only ultimate cold can produce colossal heat," the astronomer replied calmly. "Cold is a form of extremely latent energy; in a sense it is the negative force of combined negative and positive force. Our energy-projectors, housed here in this laboratory, and trained directly on the point in space we have determined, will convert that ultimate of cold energy into its exact opposite—radiant heat. As the process continues we shall gradually widen the area of our projectors' radii until the sun—which from here will appear as a large star—is the size we desire. This size is approximately one million miles in diameter."

"But surely your projectors cannot expand their radii so as to cover a million miles' width?" Axata asked amazedly.

"Certainly they can, Princess; remember that the distance away is four hundred million miles. Our streams of vibration lose nothing of their power, no matter how far they travel. The greater the distance the wider the ultimate of the beam, if one may call it such. So when this flaming gas has reached the desired width of one million miles, another type of vibration, a disruptive type, will be hurled forth, which will split masses of matter from this gas, to form planets.

"Our calculations show that there ought to be some nine planets of varying sizes, considering the actual mass of the sun itself. Naturally, these disrupted masses of gas will be hurled outward into space, but will ultimately be held by the parent gas—sun—whose mass will outweigh the entire number of planets and their moons by something like seven hundred and twenty times. Hence, it will be the center of gravitation. Indeed, our calculations have shown that some of the disrupted portions may be flung even far past the orbit of our own planet of Jir. It appears that our planet—or what remains of it after the internal gas has done its work—will lie somewhere between the paths of the first outer and the last inner planet of the sun. There will, by almost inevitable law, be four or five very large worlds to form an outer group, and four much smaller ones to form an inner group. That we know already."

"But surely, Hanzan, this terrific feat cannot be completed in four days?" Morna asked surprisedly. "Why, even from my own elementary knowledge of the cosmos I know that it requires ages for a solar system to cool down."

Hanzan smiled faintly. "A natural solar system, yes," he assented. "But with a man-made one, it is different. Let me finish explaining to you. When the nine planets have been disrupted they will hurtle in eccentric orbits round the parent body, and, if left to themselves, would continue like that for ages to come—until, being much smaller than their sun, they would gradually cool and become habitable. We, however, who can kindle heat out of zero, can also perform the reverse action and make these flaming worlds habitable within the space of a few hours. The sun itself we shall also cool down somewhat from its primary heat.

"This same action of cooling the planets will result in the masses spinning round on their own axes, at a great speed to begin with, then gradually slowing. As they do this, they will hurl forth their moons, and these moons, being smaller, will cool first, of course. You will see these gases of planets in our instruments as unformed flaming masses, at first; then, under the action of our vibrations, you will watch them gradually take on a bulging form—globes with a distended equator. Then they will become quasi round, with a round protuberance at one end. This end will finally break off and be hurled into space to become either one moon, or several, depending on whether the mass breaks or not."

The astronomer ceased for a moment. "And out of those nine worlds one, or perchance two, will be suitable for our type of life," he added quietly.

"Why not all of them?" Morna asked quickly.

"The five outer ones will be useless, for obvious reasons. Their gravitation will be too strong; their distance from the sun too great. Upon them, other natural chemical life may form. Only upon one or two of the inner planets can our synthetic race take root and begin to grow. As soon as our cosmic work is ended, we can then determine which world we shall use for our experiment. Then, across the gulf, will be hurled the brain protoplasms, male and female, despatched in separate projectiles, and guided by the mass of light vibration—light has mass, you know—eventually to strike the chosen planet, where the projectiles will break open and the protoplasms will start to grow. Also we shall send seeds of our trees and plants, which ultimately will flourish—and finally there will be a world akin to our own."

"What of the gravitational shiftings during this process?" Morna inquired. "The appearance of another solar system will cause great upheavals, surely?"

"Certainly there will be great disturbances, but we counteract that by issuing forth bracing rays of force upon distant stars. That should hold us comparatively steady. In any case, since our world is doomed it matters little; we want respite only long enough to continue our surgical work after we've made the system."

The astronomer paused. "Have I explained sufficiently?" he asked.

"Sorry to have taken so much of your time," Morna said earnestly. "We won't detain you any longer. We'll be back again tonight at sundown to witness this celestial miracle."

"It will be your duty," Hanzan returned calmly. "The entire higher circle will be present, headed by your august father. And now, if you will pardon me, I have much to do."

* * * *

With all the grandiose pomp and ceremony for which Jir was famed, the entire retinue of intellectuals who controlled the City of Science—the higher circle—filed into the vast observatory-laboratory at sundown. Varnos, Lord of Jir, and Morna's father, headed the procession—a regal, steadfast figure in robes of scarlet and gold.

Hanzan, Laznor by his side, bowed low before the ruler; then came a rustling movement among the servants as chairs were hastily placed in position for the dignitaries of the doomed planet.

Presently they were all seated. The door closed; the radium bowls blazed forth with a sudden soft yet vehement brilliance. Outside, the sun sank down in the purple banks couched to the rear of the mighty City of Science.

For a long time Hanzan stood by the window, gazing out at the slowly appearing stars. He turned and motioned to a gigantic screen occupying a large portion of the laboratory wall.

"The view screen of my reflector," he explained. "Upon this screen is projected, from my telescope, the light-waves the instrument has gathered. As your highness is aware, our object-glass is perhaps the greatest achievement in Jir. Sixteen feet wide, four feet thick, and composed of the master-element Miranium, No. 104 in our periodic table. Opaque and heavy to the eye, but transparent and magnetic to light waves, it gathers the faintest possible radiations of light to itself for a distance of ten billion miles and brings those light-waves to itself without the faintest trace of distortion or fading. Then, subsequent magnification—and we have perfect results. This instrument is now trained on the comparatively blank spot in space where we are to create our solar system. Now—"

A clicking sound followed, then the central tube of the colossal apparatus, poking its blunt, unseen head through the circular roof, glowed suddenly white, finally becoming pink. Upon the screen there appeared a dead, deep blackness.

Hanzan smiled faintly. "Space!" he explained. "The view now is purely that of the infinite. In a moment you will see our work begin."

He turned aside and rapped out orders to his waiting assistants. They took up their positions before various control boards, attached to which were numberless dynamos, generators, and other electrical and semi-electrical contrivances.

Along the floor, across the walls, in the roof, snaked and twined thick and thin cables, all heavily insulated, ending their devious and tortuous paths in six massively built machines on pedestals at the far end of the laboratory, their wide, lensed orifices pointing skyward at an angle of seventy-five degrees. Clockwork precision motors began to tick rhythmically beside them, slowly keeping them checked against Jir's natural revolution on its axis, upon the predetermined point in space.

Great springs, obviously made to stand enormous recoiling pressure, were sunken down into supports buried seven feet in a bed of metal and rhone—the heaviest and toughest stone known to Jir. Nothing had been left to chance.

Through an interval Hanzan checked up with intent, fevered earnestness upon all his calculations, and at last he nodded. A trifle dramatically he raised his hand as a signal, and immediately the six assistants, each controlling a switchboard attached to an energy-projector, depressed master switches. A monstrous column of green light rose from energy-promoting mechanism from which the power was drawn, and then slowly faded and expired.

The floor shook with power; the energy surged unseen along the devious cables provided and entered the projectors. Immediately six independent beams of blinding green stabbed into the darkness outside, passing through the wide-flung window opening, and continued to blaze forth with undiminished brilliance.

Hanzan nodded in satisfaction and glanced at the telescopic screen. It was already suffusing with green—a fact which caused, the intent Morna to ask:

"So soon, Hanzan? I understood the fastest known velocity is that of light, at one hundred and eighty-six thousand miles a second. Even that would take roughly forty-five of our minutes to travel four hundred million miles. Yet we are seeing the green beams almost immediately after projection."

"Quite so," Hanzan responded. "Light is not by any means the fastest known speed. I grant that it possesses the fastest velocity of its particular class of radiation, but there are infinitely faster speeds. Take gravitation—it makes itself felt instantly over any given distance. As for these beams, they move at a velocity of approximately two billion miles a second—nor is that the fastest known speed."

The convergence of the six beams of energy resulted finally in one almost blinding spot of green fire being concentrated on the utter blackness of space. For a long time, as it seemed, nothing changed. The machinery in the observatory hummed on without pause; the projectors slowly turned in their clock-motivated bearings.

At last Hanzan uttered a triumphant cry, pointing to the screen.

Out of the deadness, the frozen vacuum of space, there was gradually forming a bright, intensely blue-white spot, containing indeed the vaguest suggestion of violet. With the passing of the minutes, and the concentrated force of the energy-projectors, the spot grew, became an uneven, flaming mass of superheated energy.

Hanzan turned away from the screen for a moment and pressed a button. Immediately there fell over the screen a shield of purple glass, which mitigated the almost eye-paralyzing intensity of the glare.

As the gas grew and expanded, additional layers of purple glass were dropped, into position, until at length the audience was gazing through no fewer than eight sheets of protective covering at a dazzling mass now covering the whole screen.

It was no longer possible to see how far the gas had spread; its edges had overrun the screen's limits.

Therefore, Hanzan stood silent, eyes fixed upon a chronometer on the wall, only glancing occasionally at the swirling, turbulent mass of energy and unthinkable heat that his remarkable energy-projectors had produced.

"It is fortunate indeed that the gas is so rapid in growth the instant the first spark of energy has been kindled," he remarked, turning. "For it to swell to the desired size of one million miles' diameter is not a long task—about sixty minutes at the most, expanding and eating up void as it does."

He turned aside for a moment and spoke into a communicator. "Brace beams firmly fixed?" he asked curtly; then nodded in satisfaction at the answer. "At that rate there is nothing to fear from gravitative upheavals," he commented, turning again. "Otherwise, there is mass and energy enough in the void now to blow our world out of its orbit."

Minutes passed on; the chronometer hand flicked silently round its white-faced dial. Another shield of purple glass dropped into position with soft emphasis.

Hanzan raised his hand. "Cease!" he commanded.

Simultaneously the six projectors discontinued their emanations. The massive generating engines whined down the scale of sound to a standstill. Quietness fell.

Hanzan looked impressively at his ruler. "Your highness, a sun is born," he said solemnly. "Now for the children of the sun!"

Again he swung around on his assistants. "Force beams—immediately!" he rapped out, and became once more a quick, agile figure, full of earnest, scientific intent.

The conversion of the projectors was but the work of a moment. Reversing contacts were switched onto the power generators, and the energy that formerly had kindled incomprehensible heat, from equally incomprehensible cold, was altered in vibration so that it now hurtled forth as a battering-ram of destructive, disintegrating power. Six beams of green light again stabbed from the projectors and, as before, appeared almost immediately on the sheathed screen, now only faintly visible against the glaring photosphere of the sun.

The instant they struck that seething, boiling effulgence of heat, mighty masses of flaming gas spewed out into space as though flung with a Titan's hand, pieces that immediately vanished beyond the screen's width. Hanzan made a few rapid adjustments with experienced fingers and revealed the sun at a farther distance, where it was possible to behold it now with three, flaming masses of disrupted gas swinging round in a zigzagging, drunken circle, trying to fly off into the void, but held by the infinitely greater power of the parent mass.

The force beams were cut off, and then hurtled forth again, twice more—and twice more writhing gas shot forth into emptiness, to even greater distances. Indeed, five of the masses hurtled so far away that it began to appear as if they would career off into space, impelled by their initial momenta, never to return. As they vanished from the screen's view, Hanzan shrugged his shoulders.

"Evidently our dream of nine worlds will not be fulfilled," he said somberly. "Five of the glowing masses have shot beyond the gravitative reach, I'm afraid. It all depends on whether the sun's attraction is sufficiently strong to hold them before they get out of control." He looked back at the screen. "Four of the masses are safe, close to the sun," he said thoughtfully. "I should say the farthest one is about one hundred and thirty-three million miles from the sun, and the nearest about thirty-six million miles."

He turned to his assistants once more. "Release the cooling beams!" he ordered, and again the green beams shot forth, now changed to the exactly opposite vibration from that which they had started with. With their usual unthinkable speed they reached the sun, and began to concentrate upon it with unremitting power.

After a time the sun seemed to become dimmer. Quietly Hanzan moved his buttons, and the layers of purple shields vanished one after the other, leaving presently the clear view. It became instantly manifest that, while the four newborn planets, moving in their intoxicated orbits, were blue-white, the sun had changed to a snow-white shade, and, as the cooling vibrations continued, altered very slowly to a vaguely greenish white, then down to flaming yellow-white, the yellow being somewhat predominant.

"That will do," Hanzan said, and then suddenly switched over two of his purple shields.

The glare rendered less powerful, the astonished audience distinctly beheld the actual disk of the sun itself; no longer an unformed gas, but a blazing circle.

"If we had no atmosphere on Jir we should undoubtedly be treated to the sight of superb solar prominence and pearly corona," Hanzan commented. "And in case the changing of colors puzzles you, let me explain that the ultimate of solar heat is blue-white, as you saw at first. As it cools, it goes down to yellow-white, as you see it now. As centuries roll on, allowing the sun to take a natural course of cooling, it will become golden-yellow, then slowly down through decreasing heat stages until it is red, and at last—extinct. The sun is now fully created, has a form, and a vaguely determinable revolution. The planets, being smaller, will be much simpler tasks."

With that he turned his attention to the four worlds, using two force beams apiece on the two larger ones, and one each on the smaller ones—the one nearest the sun and the one farthest away.

It was particularly astounding to the audience to watch how those flawlessly guided fingers of energy molded the formless gases across the bottomless reaches of the cosmos. Slowly, yet with inevitable precision, the aberrant, erring gases were subdued from their blazing, gassy state—through all the stages of cooling—down from the blue-white to the red, then down to the solidifying state, a process which revealed the forming of the planets even as the work continued.

Mighty, internal upheavals engulfed them all; they swelled and reared with terrific inner convulsions; threw up colossal mountain ranges and mighty columns of impenetrable scalding vapors.

The moons of these forming worlds, too, presently broke off and fell into orbits around their parent worlds.

So the work went on, but so intent was Hanzan that he overlooked one vital thing. Concentrating on the two largest planets, he forgot to halt the work on the two smaller ones, with the result that by the time the two center globes had become steaming worlds, entirely to his satisfaction, the smaller ones had become already brittle, dry, and almost devoid of water vapor. Their natural warmth had practically vanished.

Quite abruptly the astronomer comprehended this and gave a violent start. The order to halt at once followed.

"Oh, a thousand pities!" he groaned in self-condemnation. "Out of four fine worlds I've ruined two! I forgot, in the intensity of the moment, that the smaller masses would cool more rapidly. This means that, forever more, they will be infinitely further ahead in their surface conditions.

"And another tragedy, too!" he added, after a moment's thought, "Something, somewhere, has upset the path of the energy beam concentrated on the smallest planet, nearest the sun. See, its axial tilt is all wrong! It means that it will forever turn one face to the sun and the other to the void. Oh, what a bungle I have made of everything!"

"If I may say so, sir," said Morna presently, who had been closely studying the screen, "the same thing has happened to the vibration concentrated on the second planet from the sun, as well. See, that one also is moving round with one face to the sun. The top of its axis, like the smaller one, is inclined directly to the sun."

Hanzan gazed in speechless despair at the four molded planets, turning slowly on their axes—at a speed which through the ages would slow down by solar and tidal drags—at varying distances from the sun. A long study of the second planet confirmed Morna's remark. The master scientist grunted his utter and heartfelt disgust.

"That leaves only one!" he snapped out. "Two are useless because of axial eccentricity. We'll call the nearest one 'Mercury,' meaning our ancient term for 'Mistake.' The second, also spoiled, we'll call 'Venus,' our term for 'Nothing.' The fourth one has been too far advanced in the cooling stage to be of use, so we will name it 'Mars'— 'Outcast.' The center one, the third, alone remains—a warm, properly axiated world at the very dawn of its life, perfect for the propagation of our brain protoplasms. That we will call 'Earth'—or 'Home.'"

He smiled wearily. "You two, Morna—princess, have registered those names in your malleable brains and will hand them down. Probably the future race that will spring from you will find different interpretations for the names of the planets, but the original names will stay as I have given them!"

He smiled again, bitterly this time. "Five truly mighty planets missing, three ruined, and one left! And I had hoped for so much!"

"You have little justification to condemn yourself, Hanzan," said the Lord of Jir, slowly rising to his feet. "To have obtained even one fruitful world out of your experiment is to your undying credit. You—"

He broke off and looked up with a startled expression on his face as suddenly, from outside, there came the beating tumult and surging of a sudden mighty wind. The mass of the observatory began to shake slightly in the grip of an all-powerful gale.

"What is that?" Morna asked, startled.

Without waiting for an answer he dashed to the window. The moment he arrived there he stood stupefied; silently the others came up behind him.

Incredibly near, as it seemed, hurtling through the star-studded sky, was a mighty flaming mass of gas, keeping on a line with the horizon. Farther away still, passing into remoteness, were three other similar masses, moving at a like speed.

"Great heavens above! The missing planets!" Hanzan jerked out huskily. "They have been flung to an unthinkable distance, have taken this long to get here, but the sun has held them! Thank the gods that they must have crossed the opposite side of our world, reducing its surface to cinders with the unthinkable heat. We, on this side, in our impregnable city, are comparatively safe. Even as it is the disturbances from the other side of our planet are causing mighty atmospheric upheavals here."

With that he swung around on his assistants and gave them an abstruse formula to work out. The moment their computations were complete they altered the position of the energy-projectors and, at a word from their master, released six cooling beams.

"This may be successful—it may not," Hanzan muttered, watching the blinding mass near the horizon. "Such colossal bodies will take a great deal of cooling, but we can only try. We managed the sun, so we can manage these smaller ones, perhaps, though, of course, we didn't try to reduce the sun to a solid state. I am training three on this giant nearest us, two on the next one, and one on the third. The fourth will have to cool down through time of its own accord. Where the fifth has gone I don't know."

Steadily, the tremendous force of the cooling vibrations began to take effect, assisted to a certain extent by the great distance from the primal luminary, the sun. In dead silence, heedless of the thunderings and buffetings of the hot and scorching gale thundering through the city, the audience watched.

Then presently came a remarkable occurrence in connection with the second planet.

Ten moons had been flung from its cooling bulk— the first two truly gigantic masses, when suddenly these monstrous pieces came into violent collision, obviously by some gravitational eccentricity that it was not in Hanzan's power to prevent.

The result was remarkable. Eight moons were left, struggling to maintain their orbits round the now cooling major body, when the cooling rays struck dead in the center of the two interlocked, flaming moons. Almost immediately they began to cool, but so mighty was the gravitation of the planet itself, and so strong the pull of the remaining eight satellites, that the cooling, disintegrated pieces collapsed even further, until at last they were a cloudy mist of microscopic bodies—as compared to the planet—that finally had spread themselves with some unaccountable centrifugal action round the parent body, forming at last into vaguely understandable rings, only visible because they were very slightly tilted toward the Jirian observers.

"Incredible!" Hanzan breathed. "A beauteous creation indeed—finally it will turn into a ringed planet. An astronomical freak! We will name it 'Saturn'—'Rings'." A troubled frown crossed his brow. "This nearer monster is indeed taking a long time to cool," he muttered. "See— it is still bulging around the equator, not even properly solid. Certainly it *is* solidifying, for its nine moons have been given birth. Perhaps if we stopped concentrating only on one area it might help. One big red spot there is solidified where our rays have touched—you see? Between the drifting clouds? But the rest of the planet is still molten." He fell to thought.

"That one must be 'Jupiter,' your highness," he announced. "That means 'Mighty.' As for the third one we'll name it 'Uranus'—'Lost.' The farthest one, which we have not attempted to solidify, we can name 'Neptune'— 'Outermost.' If the fifth one should ever be discovered it must be known as 'Pluto'—'Stranger.' Yes, I must give the order for more universal concentration on Jupiter."

He turned actively aside to give the order. But suddenly the gale rose in all its screaming, devastating fury.

The window glass, before which the party was standing, cracked into a thousand splinters—glass which had withstood three thousand years.

The floor heaved mightily with sudden turbulent undercurrents. From somewhere came the sound of roaring and rumbling, as of some behemoth flood of water.

"Another groundquake!" Hanzan shouted at last. "The disturbances have caused yet another outbreak of that fatal inner gas. We—"

He staggered a pace, then stopped appalled as quite abruptly a monstrous fissure appeared in the observatory ceiling. Immediately afterward one vast supporting pillar cracked in two, as though of tinder consistency, hurling great masses of stone and metal into the midst of the priceless instruments.

"Quick—out of here!" Morna exclaimed, clutching Axata to him. "The whole place is falling in!"

His words were only too true. The violent ground tremors, caused undoubtedly by the annihilating force of the atomic gas within the planet, became even more constant as the minutes passed. Instrument after instrument smashed to irreparable ruin; electricity flashed and flared as wires were snapped. The vast telescopic reflector presently snapped in two and dropped amid the ruins of the six projector switchboards.

Everything became an incomprehensible jumble of debris on the quaking, shivering floor. In the midst of it all Hanzan stood like one stunned, suddenly bereft of the power to think. Then he was firmly seized by the Lord of Jir and piloted strongly and resolutely from the doomed laboratory into the splintering corridor outside.

Staggering and lurching, they at last gained the open, struggling through the collapsing doorway and down the steps.

Then abruptly—calmness!

As suddenly as it had begun the quaking ceased. There came little thuds and bumps as detached pieces of masonry fell to the ground in the sudden ensuing silence. The mad upheavals of the atmosphere passed. Clouds there never were in this perfectly organized atmosphere of a master planet, but dust there had been in vast quantities. Now the dust was gently settling to the ground again, allowing the stars and the half-cooled mass of Jupiter, sinking below the horizon, to shine forth clearly and without tremor.

Little lights that had been extinguished came up in different parts of the city. To the left the beauteous place was a shambles, but to the right there seemed to be but little change.

"An unfinished task!" muttered Hanzan regretfully. "Jupiter—I cooled only one spot to be habitable, and the rest, molten! Look at his cloud banks! And in the far future our perpetuated race will wonder what that red spot means, and not until they reach the end of their course and incidentally attain the same standard of intellect as we have now, will they realize that an accident caused it. I am disgusted! In the normal span it will take millions of years for a world that large to cool—it will outlive even our chosen planet Earth."

"Why worry over that, Hanzan?" asked the Lord of Jir quietly. "We have done much—be satisfied. Come to my abode and be rested—if anything remains of my abode," he added with grim reflection.

"I am not so troubled about that; I am wondering if the surgical laboratories are still safe," remarked Laznor, gazing over Hanzan's shoulder. "Upon their safety rests the only hope of our race being able to continue its knowledge, for there are housed the projectiles to fire the protoplasms to Earth,"

"Yes," agreed Hanzan quietly, then as though following some thought of his own: "Jir's life indeed grows short..."

IV.

Investigation revealed that the ground disturbances had taken place almost entirely in the left ramparts of the City of Science, and that portion had been reduced to complete ruin, burying hundreds of unfortunates in the midst of the debris. To the right, it was found that curiously little havoc had been wrought—the lord's palace and the huge surgical laboratories were untouched, save for slight collapses that could be easily rectified. The Earth projectors and amazing instruments for the creation of artificial protoplasm were untouched.

The day following, their last day of life on Jir, Morna and Axata went out together to take what they knew was perhaps their last farewell. Their path took them, almost unconsciously, to the left of the city, through the very midst of the ruins, until at length they came to a heaped-up pile of boulders at the foot of a disintegrated cliff. With mute accord they seated themselves in the full blaze of their very-near sun.

"The last day," said Morna quietly, at length. "I find it hard to believe."

"It is not so much that that I am worrying over, Morna," Axata replied, her chin resting thoughtfully on her hand. "It is the fact that our parting from each other will cause sorrow, and as our brains are so malleable to impressions, that sorrow will be handed down to our successors. Think—men and women capable of expressing sorrow! An outrage to intelligence, is it not?"

"Maybe," Morna admitted. "Frankly, I don't think we are going to produce such a wonderful race, after all. We know already, from what our brains have impressed upon them, that the future race will know both sorrow and love—for we both love each other. Sorrow and love are two big hindrances to progress."

"I wonder—" the girl began thoughtfully, then she looked round in puzzled surprise as a grinding, roaring growl made itself evident behind her.

With astounding swiftness, a mighty fissure appeared in the ground to the rear, from which belched forth enormous columns of dense sulphuric steam and smoke.

"Morna!" she managed to shriek hoarsely, for the first time in her life revealing the forgotten element—terror.

She proceeded no further. The rock on which she was half seated lurched backward into the gulf, carrying her helplessly threshing form with it. Her screams echoed through the chasm.

Instantly Morna was on his feet, the sweat of utter horror breaking out on his face. Never in his life had he known such fright. The girl had gone. True, the fissure seemed now to have ceased widening, but— No! There was another gap breaking forth in the distance. Everywhere, the surface of the planet was being rent apart by the pent-up gas that no longer could be withheld by walls of stone and metal.

"Axata!" Morna bellowed desperately, at the top of his voice, struggling forward on hands and knees to the edge of the smoking chasm. "Axata!" But his voice only rang in the emptiness.

He struggled forward again, lying on his face, and peered down into the depths. He could make out now that it was not a sheer drop. There were countless ledges and crevices. The only hope was that the girl had not been hurled outward, for if so she must undoubtedly have plunged into the dark unknown below, into the very white-hot center of the tortured planet.

Intense fear for her safety was on Morna now and, with the fear, a curious, seething hatred—that the planet should have taken from him so ruthlessly the one creature in all Jir for whom he had love and affection.

For a space he lay gazing down, forming numberless conjectures. Perhaps the boulder that went with her had pinned her under its crushing weight lower down—had smashed the life out of her. Perhaps in her headlong drop into the chasm she had been caught between rocks from which it would be impossible to extricate her. Or perhaps—

Morna did not surmise any further. With a sudden fixity of purpose he clambered over the rough edge of the chasm and began cautiously to edge his way down the precipitous, newly riven slope.

It was dangerous work, he soon discovered. The pathway was strewn with countless loose stones and pebbles, and frequently he missed his footing on the narrow, downwardly sloping declivity. One slip, and undoubtedly he would be hurled into the smoky enigma below.

Slowly and with infinite care he progressed, until at length he came to a wider and more substantial ledge.

He advanced a few paces, searching with frantic eyes through the smoke, shouting the girl's name, until presently his roving gaze caught sight of something white amidst the steamy riot of crumbled stones. In an instant he had reached the spot.

"Axata!" he breathed, in hushed horror.

She was lying half buried beneath a mass of loose stones, covered to her waist. Streaks of blood were upon her arms and face; her raiment was torn and slashed. Quietly, dumbly, Morna went on his knees beside her and raised her head in his arms. No sign of life came into the ashen face. At last he listened for her heart, and to his unbounded joy detected its slow beating. She still lived, then.

With renewed energy he set to work to fling away the stones that covered her, looking in horror during his operations as he found one heavy boulder that lay across her legs. He uncovered her at last, and despite his strength of character his eyes suddenly brimmed with tears at the sight of the girl's crushed and lacerated limbs.

Again that mad, almost ungovernable rage came within him—that the planet should so maltreat and belabor that which he loved. Then the rage abruptly changed into pity. Silently he picked up her limp body in his powerful arms and set about the task of climbing the slope once more—to reach the top, a ragged, blood-streaked giant, half an hour later.

With all the speed at his command he set out for the city, shouting against the planet and destiny as he went.

* * * *

Laznor stood completely aghast when he beheld the bleeding ruin of a girl that Morna placed reverently and miserably on the operating table in the master surgeon's laboratory. Instantly he came forward and stared at the girl as though unable to believe the testimony of his eyes.

"What in the name of the gods is this?" he demanded.

Briefly Morna explained. "She still lives," he concluded dully. "What can you do?"

Laznor thought for a moment, then he applied to the wounds an ointment that instantly stopped the profuse bleeding. The administration of a complicated opiate into a vein of the girl's arm had the effect of causing her to relax gently, as though falling into a deep sleep. For a long time Laznor stood surveying her in silence, then his deep-set eyes looked up into those of the disheartened youth before him.

"Tragedy!" he breathed sorrowfully, shaking his massive head. "Tragedy! I might have known it; we are usurping the Creator's power. Last night, the same shadow of ill luck stalked us. One planet out of nine! The observatory was reduced to dust! And now this! *This*—to affect the whole future of women! Axata will live only a few hours longer, and that life can only be under an opiate. The only thing to do is to make the brain-protoplasm projection earlier than we intended. Ah, a thousand pities!"

"How does this so alter everything? For future women?" Morna asked listlessly.

"Is it not obvious, boy?" Laznor demanded, almost impatiently. "Axata's condition will mean that her brain has taken the impressions of pain, of misery, of weakened physical condition, and lack of nervous control. It means that the women who will follow after her will be weaker than the men—will know the meaning of pain, will be prone to hysteria and nervous excitement—instead of the calm, resourceful women I had planned. Always will they be weaker than the man."

Laznor's shoulders drooped in the profound dejection of a man who has made a mighty struggle and failed to attain his objective. Presently he looked up again with curiously lackluster eyes.

"And you, my boy. You also will hand down to men the meaning of fear, of hate, of primitive passion for your mate. Upon my soul, it is atavism! Nothing more or less! All we have strived for—wiped out! We shall make a race—yes; but it will take until the end of Earth's life for it to be what we desire. Until that time it will be a world populated by men and women who know fear, love, and hate. Complex, barbarous beings. By all the gods of the cosmos! If only I had not made your brains so malleable! Still—it is, as it is. The Earth projection will take place, badly marred though it will be."

Laznor stopped and looked at the slowly breathing girl. "I must set to work immediately," he said in sudden alarm. "She has less time to live than I thought. And I must tell you, Morna, that she will never again recover consciousness. She has spoken her last word to you in this life."

The master surgeon looked at the young man's unhappy face with his understanding eyes, then went on more gently, "But when the gulfs of time and space have been bridged—who knows but that you may hear her voice again?"

With that he turned aside and, with the curious detachment so remarkable to the scientists of Jir, became immersed in his work, a trifle impatient at the short notice under which he was forced to proceed.

Morna, dazed by the rapidity of events, stood silently by the girl's side, holding her limp hand in his. Absently his eyes continued to stare at a curious crossed scar on the girl's left forearm, a deeply chiseled but now blood-less laceration in the distinct form of an X, manifestly occasioned by the ruthless stones that had all but crushed the life out of her. In some odd way that scar fascinated his mind unduly. He pondered upon it—then suddenly he was awakened from abysmal preoccupation by the voice of his father.

"I cannot begin to express my regret for this occurrence, my son," Varnos said quietly, placing a steadying hand on Morna's shoulder. "It seems, even as Laznor has stated, that misfortune is dogging our efforts from start to finish."

"Yes; it does seem so," Morna admitted; then with an effort he aroused himself, admitting his surprise at discovering the surgical laboratory now contained not only his father and retinue, but also Hanzan, and several assistant surgeons and projectile electricians, all working under Laznor's orders.

"I was summoned here by Laznor to witness this last scientific experiment in the history of Jir," Varnos explained, reading the unspoken question in Morna's eyes. "It is my will to be with you to the end—Morna."

"Thank you, father." Morna turned aside, swallowing something in his throat, and with the others began to watch the experiment take on form.

Two surgeons, after making certain that Axata was completely anaesthetized, set to work with electrical knives and saws, performing the most skillful skull and brain operation that had ever been seen. Two incisions were made in the forehead, and into the apertures were fixed two flexible tubes, leading to a monstrous glass container I of dull-yellow consistency.

In grim silence the Lord of Jir watched the proceedings from under his heavy brows; Laznor moved rapidly up and down, intent only on the satisfactory outcome of his dangerous yet admirably courageous work.

"The protoplasm—female element number one!" Laznor commanded at last, and within the yellow glass container there appeared suddenly a bubbling, saffron mass, forced up from air-tight chambers below by some pressure system. For a long time the curiously repulsive, jelly-like liquid boiled and eddied, until at length it half-filled the container. The pressure force was removed, and with the calm detachment of an expert Laznor surveyed the protoplasm pensively.

"Excellent!" he commented at length. "Very healthy indeed! You understand, your highness that the tubes which are affixed to the centers of the Princess' brain will draw forth by magnetic power given and predetermined cells from the cerebrum? These cells will pass through the tubes by suction and down into the protoplasm. Then an electric current will magnetize those cells, which will ultimately mean they will all join together again by mutual attraction. That, finally, will result in the independent impressions becoming formed into one composite whole.

"Inevitably our specially prepared female protoplasm will seek its opposite in chemical attraction—the male protoplasm—which will of course, be impregnated with Morna's brain cells. So, gradually, as the law of evolution goes on, intelligent life will arrive, as cell by cell accrues, and more knowledge, stored within those cells, is released. I fear me the process may be delayed somewhat because, in a sense, the race we are creating will have two things to accomplish—one, to use the impressions they have to begin with, and the other, to use fresh cells to cope with immediate experiences. However, that will be their task. We have given the fundamental—the rest is purely growth and expansion. Now—continue!" he ordered, turning to the assistants.

They turned to their tasks, and the curious suction machines set to work. Nothing was apparent to the eye, however, despite the length of time the engines continued their throbbing.

The girl on the table seemed presently to stiffen. Something of the limpness that had been upon her changed to rigidity. Laznor shot her a quick glance, then raised his hand for the machinery to be stopped.

"Only just in time," he said slowly. "The transference has been completed with not a second to spare, and, quite naturally, it has brought death sooner than we expected, considering Axata's weakened condition. The cells are fairly healthy, as it happens, but they will carry the unwanted impressions of which I told you."

"You—you mean that Axata is—is dead?" Morna asked huskily.

The master surgeon nodded gravely. "Yes, my son. But within that protoplasm is her brain. You saw nothing; the cells as we remove them are too small for visibility. Only by calculation is it possible to know when the work is ended. There, in that container, is the protoplasm from which the women of the planet we have called Earth will ultimately spring!"

"Oh—it's horrible!" Morna muttered, turning away.

"You are overwrought, my son. Our work is supreme!" Laznor returned steadily. "We are perpetuating knowledge. There cannot be a greater achievement than that!"

"Yes, but you don't love Axata as I do!" Morna half shouted, swinging around. "You cannot understand my emotions! All this! It's—ghastly!"

"It is not in a surgeon of Jir to understand love or kindred emotions of the nerves," replied the aged genius with unshatterable calm. "To us, Axata is—or was—a woman, and therefore capable of being the progenitor of a race. Science does not admit love or pity; three thousand years of scientific progress have drilled such sentiments out of us. Science is a calculated art, based on immovable and flawless fundamentals."

So saying, Laznor turned aside and under his directions the brain-impregnated protoplasm was pumped into yet another glass container. Here it underwent, for a time, the electrical radiations of which the surgeon had spoken, then the entire mass was emptied by a small vacuum tube into a cube of glass a foot square. Curious rays of pink and green began to play upon it from amid the laboratory's numberless instruments; at length Laznor picked the cube up and looked at it thoughtfully.

"Inside this box is the perfect vacuum," he commented, "and the walls, though they appear thin and transparent, are capable of standing the pressure of the flight through space and the infinite cold. But upon striking Earth the box will snap apart—it is designed to do so—and the protoplasm will be released into the warmth and succulence of our man-made planet."

"It is well," said the Lord of Jir steadily, watching with deep interest.

Morna gazed at the box with troubled eyes for a moment, then he started violently as he beheld two of the assistant surgeons lift Axata's body unceremoniously from the table and dump it heavily onto an adjoining one. The action aroused within him again that semi-dormant sense of helpless passion.

"You've no right to treat Axata like that!" he exploded abruptly and, striding forward, seized the surprised Laznor by the shoulder. "You hear me, Laznor?"

"My son—steady!" the old man commanded sternly. "When will you realize that the body of itself is nothing? When it is dead it ceases to be! Only the brain, the mind alone, counts! You see there a corpse; there is no need to treat it with reverence—that is better left to the primitive little minds. A corpse is useless when the life has gone. It only awaits a disintegrating ray to destroy it before it spreads infection from mortification. Morna, be sensible! You are a child of Jir, and son of the Lord Varnos."

Morna nodded stupidly. "All right. I'm sorry. I'm afraid I'm unstrung. In fact—"

He did not finish his sentence. The master surgeon had turned away and was directing the operation of the Earth-projectile machine. Quietly Morna moved forward to watch, by the side of his regal father.

The gleaming box was placed, with infinite care and reverence, in the heart of a curiously wrought, tube-like instrument, and the keen eyes of Laznor watched the needles upon the dials that showed when the box was in position. A length he nodded, and the aperture through which the box had be« lowered was sealed up.

"Continue," he instructed calmly and stood back.

The electricians turned to the controls and rapidly moved their various switches and plugs into position. An instant later a terrific report boomed through the laboratory and the projectile cannon shot backward on its massive recoil springs. Smoke that had a tang of ozone in it curled gently around the nostrils of the watchers.

"So, your highness, the female element has gone," Laznor said quietly, bowing. "It will reach Earth, according to our calculations, in about one hundred and eighty-four hours. Next will come Morna. And after him, the trifling job of sending forth the smaller projectiles that will contain the seeds from which plants will ultimately spring. Now, Morna—if you are ready?"

For an instant Morna hesitated then he inclined his head in sudden complete composure.

"I am prepared," he answered quietly. "Continue!"

"My son—" the Lord of Jir began, striding forward with outstretched hands, then he staggered slightly, as did all in the laboratory beneath a terrific, rending concussion. The metal floor shook violently.

"Seismic disturbances continuing," commented Hanzan grimly looking out of the window. "It appears that the destruction of Jir is coming more rapidly than we expected, probably by the crust on the other side being so weakened by the passage of the giant planets last evening. Through this window I can see chasms appearing in every direction. Jir has only a few hours more to live."

"Proceed with the work—quickly!" Laznor ordered. "We must succeed, otherwise our whole scheme is useless."

Instructions were quickly issued, and Morna laid himself on the table to await the anaesthetic. He was conscious of the fact that the floor and table were vibrating mightily as he lay there.

There came a hissing note. The male protoplasm began to bubble within the containers.

Then Laznor came quietly forward, a complicated hypodermic syringe in his hand. He stood for a moment with it poised over Morna's bared and sinewy arm.

"Goodbye, my son," he said very quietly. "May the gods protect you!"

Morna swung his gaze around to meet the steadfast eyes of his father, whose arm was raised in the Jirian salutation of deepest respect.

A stab! Morna felt his arm tingle violently, then the laboratory and all it contained—the watching faces, the mighty instruments, the whole area of knowledge and super-science, all vanished in a common blur of gray, which rapidly deepened, fold by fold, into profoundest black.

V.

Morna felt that he had dropped headlong into an infinite void. For a moment he saw the stars, then his mind was, for a space, incapable of thinking, anything.

This phase was followed by a reassertion of knowledge, of a vision of stars and planets, of a world that steamed and contained weird flora and fauna. He caught transient glimpses of unformed creatures that writhed and wriggled nauseatingly in algal slime—little more than advanced amoeba on the muddy, filthy shore of a steaming newborn ocean. Cliffs rose up from this shore in impregnable upward reaches of friendless gray.

The vision passed. He beheld more mountain ranges, colossal and unbelievable in their size, and nestling jungles at their feet, of similarly massive proportions. Then, for another interval, he gazed briefly upon creatures of hair and boundless muscle; then upon men and sometimes women with faces that were rudimentarily human. Once in his travels he fancied he fell from a treetop—a long, dizzying flight—and crashed into darkness at the bottom.

Again he took up the amazing thread of time, tracing its ramifications and devious, twining paths through infinity, until he beheld a cooler world, a world where the days and nights were obviously of longer duration. The jungles, too, vanished at length, taking with them visions of gargantuan, repulsive beasts. There seemed now to be a distinct division between human beings and hairy creatures.

So onward his thoughts flew—thoughts now, and not remembrance—until at length he beheld the first signs of man's handiwork, saw the first dwellings, saw them enlarge. Evanescent and mysterious, there rose up before him mighty conquests and supreme vanquishments. War, destruction, famine, and death, striding, ruthless and blazingly flamboyant in their varied arrays, across the face of a miraculously changing planet.

Time and time again he would meet black patches that were meaningless. Hundreds of times he met them and, as he went on, thousands on tens of thousands of times, until he lost count of the intervals.

So onward—ever onward! Until, out of the unformed obscurity of it all there began to emerge things which he vaguely understood. Humans—natural creatures—men and women, sometimes children. For a flashing instant he saw the faces of his mother and father. Then came a sudden fog; it deepened. Blackness!

With infinite caution he opened his eyes, aware for the first time that he was breathing hard. Vainly he tried to remember what he had been seeing and failed. His memory was a complete blank, except for the experiences of his own immediate existence since his birth in the village twenty-seven years before. Nothing remained in his consciousness of a time before that.

His eyes beheld a small round face and bald head surmounting it—another one, a girl's, framed in fair, wispy hair, rose up eagerly, compellingly, beside it. Behind the heads and faces were peculiar mechanisms and half-drawn blinds.

"Daddy, he lives!" the girl shouted, in sudden mad ecstasy. "Oh, it is too wonderful! You've succeeded in your experiment, and he is unharmed!"

Lee Carnforth blinked a trifle dazedly as the girl suddenly flung her arms around his neck and smothered his face in affectionate, fervent kisses. Still groping through the puzzlement that clouded his brain, he sat up, and with the action remembrance of immediate events returned to him.

"Mary!" he exclaimed eagerly. "Oh—Mary!"

And for a moment the two were locked in each other's embrace.

Dr. Ainsworth coughed primly.

"My boy—how do you feel?" He assisted the young man from the table.

"Never better in my life," the young man replied, flexing his arms. "Well, has anything happened? I mean, did your stunt work, or haven't we started yet?"

"But, dear, after all you did, surely you—" Mary began, but her father silenced her with a look.

Then he turned to face Lee squarely. "Tell me, Lee, don't you remember your experiences in the City of Science on the planet Jir; remember rescuing the Princess Axata from the chasm; remember the projection of the brain-impregnated protoplasm into space to Earth?" he asked steadily.

Lee gazed at him with blank eyes. "What on earth are you talking about?" he asked in amazement. "I don't remember anything, except getting on this table. Then—then all went black for a moment, and here I am again."

Dr. Ainsworth nodded slowly. "It is quite obvious that when the cell-deadening effect is removed, the memory stored in the under cells completely and absolutely vanishes—is buried," he commented thoughtfully. "I expected that would happen, and to guard against that contingency I took a talking film of all your experiences from start to finish, and, Lee, you had enough experiences to cause me to use up nearly fifteen one-thousand-foot reels of film." He waved his hands to the camera and microphone, facing the now lifeless brain-vibration screen.

"You mean I actually did do something?" Lee demanded in astonishment.

"Far more than that, my boy. You are the cause of all men being on Earth at all!"

Lee looked at the doctor a trifle doubtfully, then a smile came to his face. At length he exploded with laughter. "Always up to your tricks!" he managed to gasp out at last, through his tears. "That's the funniest thing I've heard yet." He became suddenly serious. "Now do I get Mary?"

For an instant the doctor hesitated. A strange expression settled on his round but earnest face. "This evening I want you to come here at six sharp and be prepared to stay for some time. In that time, with intervals, I shall have the whole film of your adventures projected for you. During what is left of today I shall have the film developed in my dark room. Then, when you have seen it, you shall have my answer concerning Mary."

* * * *

Lee arrived punctually at six o'clock and was immediately seized upon by Mary, who led him into the doctor's own private little theater at the rear of his home. The doctor's own manservant had, for the evening, been commandeered as projectionist. What he was destined to think of the film was a matter for silent debate.

"Now, my boy," said the scientist pleasantly, as he entered, "make yourself quite comfortable, and learn what happened when I sent your mind back through time."

Lee nodded, still vaguely amused, and then turned to watch the screen as the lights went down.

So, for a space of nearly four and half hours, the reels went on—certain trivial details being omitted, but the whole thing pieced together gave, of course, a perfect reproduction of the entire adventure—and Lee, at first incredulous, became gradually spellbound and not a little startled, particularly at hearing voices that had spoken long before the Earth itself had been born. An entire adventure recorded from the impressions originally taken by his own optic and auditory nerves.

At the end of the reels he sat in silence in the restored light, baffled, bemused. Presently he sought the faintly smiling eyes of the doctor.

"I can't remember a thing about it," he admitted, "but all the same it must have been I—Morna. I, then, am the progenitor of all the males of the human race."

"Exactly," the doctor assented quietly. "Let me explain a thing or two. As you went backward from this time you experienced void and saw nothing of the Earth. The reason for that was because you were, if you follow me, thinking *backward,* therefore as each impression was a *former* idea, your knowledge was proportionately lesser. Result—nothing. Only the stars—eternal stars.

Ultimately, those vanished also, because you had gone right back to the point where your brain was in the protoplasm and incapable of doing any thinking at all.

"After that, knowledge began to pick up again, then you awoke on Jir prior to a brain test. But just before you got that far, you had flashing glimpses of people, of the City of Science, of rescuing Axata. That, in reverse—and enormously speeded up, were your experiences which followed *afterward*. You see? So all the ills the flesh is heir to can be traced back to the super-scientists of Jir."

"What happened before I awoke on the surgeon's table?" Lee inquired.

Ainsworth shrugged. "I don't know. I didn't force your brain back any further; I dared not risk it. Possibly, though, you could have gone backward, forever—into infinity. But that need not concern us. Now, regarding the return journey. You dropped down—notice the word 'down'—to the unintellectual state of the protoplasm, then gradually improved as the impregnated brain cells formed together. You saw yourself in the first form of life, then later as a man. In between you detected countless black gaps. Those gaps were *deaths,* where one existence ended and another started, proving my theory that a brain concept does not die with death, but is handed on in the successor, who possesses all the knowledge of his predecessor and gains more in his—or her—life span.

"One experience you had, that of falling out of a tree to death—remember the black gap at the end of the fall?—is still inherited by us, only the memory is so deep down as to be relegated to the subconscious. I refer to the falling dream. That is that memory, handed down through the eons, still there."

"Suppose—suppose a married couple have no children?" Lee ventured. "How then?"

"Well, obviously their particular state is not continued. But as their knowledge is only in common with millions of other beings, what is the result? Their failure to procreate is never noticed any more than a cupful of water from an ocean lowers the sea level."

Lee muttered: "A man-made solar system! To think our solar system isn't natural—and to think we are merely the perpetuators of Jirian knowledge, doing things we believe on our own initiative, yet which actually have been implanted to start with."

"Precisely," the doctor agreed. "Your adventure also disproves the Darwinian theory. The rightful creatures of Earth are the apes—they are the outcome of natural conditions. We humans, are really usurpers, controlling the world only because the Jirians placed us here. That is why no missing link between man and ape can be found; there isn't one! We're two distinct species—the ape, natural; and we, the perpetuators of a long-dead race.

"So, as the ages go on, we shall possess the knowledge of our creators, besides what we have accumulated for ourselves. Even the names of the planets, seemingly spontaneous from Earthly astronomers' minds, are only the names invented by Hanzan, as you heard him utter them. Truly we have found different mythological meanings for then, but what is that?"

"And the giant beasts of early days?" Lee inquired eagerly.

"Again, natural creatures of Earth. Our plants and tree are probably Jirian; we do not know if the seed projectiles were ever fired, since the record ended when your own particular experiences vanished in oblivion."

Lee sat in thought for a moment, somewhat overcome, then looked up again. "All this film has been shown in less than five hours, while I was time-traveling; yet I was there about three days and nights. How's that?"

"Merely an inconsistency of time, Lee. One can live a year in a dream, whereas the actual dream is only maybe a matter of seconds."

"Anything else? I'm all mixed up, you know—but beyond doubt I am the reincarnated son of the Lord of Jir, though I doubt if anybody would believe it!"

"Nobody would believe it," the doctor agreed, a trifle sadly. "That is the drawback to an amazing discovery. Nobody credits it! They'd say that I've made an unusual talking picture, that's all. Oh, yes; there are two other points. The ninth planet has, of course, been found, and named—as Hanzan said it would be—Pluto. And the disintegrated planet of Jir forms what we now call the asteroids, lying between the orbits of Mars and Jupiter, which is exactly where Jir once stood. Long have men puzzled over that asteroidal belt; at last we have the explanation."

"And their sun? Their artificial luminary?"

"Since it was controlled by Jir, it is obvious to assume that it expired when Jir was finally blown to atoms," the doctor replied. "Unhappily, anything that took place after your unconsciousness is not recorded, since only your brain was the interpreter. And Axata, too, had no view of it, either."

"By Jove, yes! Axata!" Lee became suddenly alert. "From the look of that film I was crazy about her. Nice girl, too," he added, half reminiscently. "It's queer, though—I love Mary a darn sight more!"

A strange smile was on the doctor's round face. "Chemical law has it that chemical through the ages will find its affinity," he commented. "Take a look at Mary's left forearm, will you?"

Wonderingly, Lee obeyed, looking closely at the girl's flesh as she pushed back her sleeve; then in the bright light he detected the faintest reminiscence of a scar, the shape of an X.

"Why, I— Good Heavens, you're not telling me that—"

"All through your passage back through time to here your mates have had the form of Axata, even when in the beast-men era," the doctor answered slowly. "It is an inevitable law that the same two protoplasmic cells that combined in the first instance must always seek out each other in other existences. Remember the brain impressions—impressions destined to leave their imprint forevermore on the physical form. Axata handed down weakness and so forth to women—you handed down fear and rage and sorrow. That brought both primeval and modern wars. But that crossed scar on Axata's wrist was the most predominant visible injury upon her after the accident, and therefore it has left its impression. And again you have found your mate—and will, until some complexity of time puts you apart and breaks the affinity forever."

"Then—then Mary is Axata, reincarnated?" Lee asked breathlessly. "Why don't you send her back in time and prove it?"

"Why do that, Lee?" the girl asked softly. "Aren't you satisfied?"

SUBCONSCIOUS

CHAPTER I

Moore Holmes was an Englishman, born and bred in Surrey, and, apart from attaining a scholarship that had led to his position as science-master in Godalming College at the age of twenty three, he had done nothing to greatly distinguish himself.

A pleasant fellow, Moore Holmes—fair, blue-eyed and interesting. By no means a gripping personality, but possessing withal a certain charm. He had planned that his life should be devoted to his career, but the arrival of chestnut-haired Una Lanister, and a violent summer thunderstorm, brought about at least two remarkable diversions in his well-ordered plans.

Late one summer evening in July 1937, Moore and Una could have been seen walking hurriedly along a Godalming country lane, hoping to escape the threatened downpour from the inky clouds above. They shouted advice to each other, to find their words drowned by the thunder that crashed overhead. The college loomed up in the distance and Moore began to speak, but hardly had he started than a blinding flash of forked lightning stabbed down directly in front of him. He stumbled and fell, conscious of a tearing pain in his left arm as he did so.

Not a second later followed the ear-shattering concussion of a heavy thunder-clap, rolling in tumbling peals to the horizon.

"Moore! Hurry up!" Una panted. "We'll get drenched!"

She turned back to where the young man was lying most un-picturesquely in the mud and shook him by the shoulder,

"...and our race must advance, Olania, no matter what happens," Moore murmured, his eyes closed and face up to the pouring rain; then he began to struggle feebly and opened his eyes with a start. Instantly his hand went to his blistered arm and torn coat sleeve.

"Moore! What's the matter?" Una demanded in his ear. "Who is Olania?"

Moore did not answer that question. Slowly he rose to his feet, rubbing his arm and forehead by turns and gazing around him as though in a daze. Presently he seemed to become aware of the solicitous girl by his side.

"Nothing—just a delusion," he said ambiguously. "Come on; let's get to the college. In case you don't know it, I've been struck by lightning. My head's singing like a kettle even yet, and my arm's burned to blazes... Let's move."

At that the girl became more attentive. "You'd better see Dr. Mason, the school doctor. I'll come along with you, if you like."

"There's no need, really. Let me see you home first—"

"Not until we've found out how much you're hurt," she answered purposefully, and nothing could change her decision. That being so, they set off through the downpour towards the bulk of the college perhaps half a mile away. Fortunately, despite the nearness and vividness of the lightning, Moore was not struck again, and some twenty minutes later, sodden and mud-bespattered, the two crawled into the school, Moore still holding his arm painfully. Under the girl's care, he made his way into the surgery of the school doctor, Doctor Mason.

He seemed much puzzled by his diagnosis of the lightning-stricken young man, and turned to the waiting, saturated girl with a baffled light in his eyes.

"The flash has done no real harm," he commented. "True it has caused a bad burn, but bandages and ointment will soon heal that. What I cannot understand are these strange delusions about which he keeps talking. Listen to him now!"

"...there is not the slightest reason to suppose but what we shall be successful," Moore murmured, eyes closed, and sitting slumped forward in the Doctor's arm chair. "I have a strange feeling, Olania, that something has happened to alter the normal way of things. A change..."

Moore's words trailed off into inaudible muttering; then he suddenly opened his eyes again to find the doctor looking down in puzzlement upon him.

"Doctor, you don't think his brain is affected, do you?" Una asked anxiously. "He isn't mentally unbalanced, or anything?"

It was clear the doctor was completely astounded. "Frankly, Miss Lanister, I do not know what on earth is the matter with him!" he confessed. "My examination shows that he is quite normal, save for the burned arm and very slight shock. And yet—Moore, how do you feel?" he asked directly, at which the young science-master rose into a sitting position.

"Not bad," he grunted. "My head still aches, and I think I've been dreaming, or something. I've seen strange, queer-looking people, talked with them. *I* don't know! It's all jumbled—confused!"

"You said something strange a moment ago—a long sentence," Mason remarked. "Can you recall it?"

Moore pondered and finally shook his head. "Oh, be hanged to it, Doc. Only a dream, that's all. I'll be all right. Here, bandage up this arm of mine will you?"

Mason nodded and quietly set about the task.

As he worked he talked.

"If you're troubled by anything curious, Moore—find your mind in any way confused do not hesitate to let me know. Only time can show how the lightning has affected you. It plays queer freaks, you know. Some people have developed sixth sense and X-ray eye-sight by being struck by lightning."

Moore smiled faintly. "Don't worry, Doc—nothing so useful has happened to me! Still, if anything does go wrong I'll look in on you, of course. Ah, that's better!" He surveyed his bandaged arm in satisfaction and drew on his coat again. "Thanks, Doc... Now Una, I insist on seeing you home. The storm seems to have cleared."

"But are you fit?" she asked anxiously.

"Of course I am! Now come on, before you catch cold..."

* * * *

Upon his return to the college, after he had taken leave of Una until the following evening, Moore found on entering his study that his headache had vanished. The discovery pleased him considerably, and to celebrate the fact he ate a more than normal supper to reassure himself there was nothing amiss with his digestive powers.

Towards midnight he retired to his room, and, adopting his usual practice, he switched on the electric light and then threw himself full length on the bed, fully clothed, to pass a few minutes in silent cogitation before the tiresome business of undressing. Lazily he took off his collar and tie, flung them on the dressing table, then, hands behind his head, he closed his eyes to think.

The instant he had closed them, however, he opened them again in sudden fright. For, when his lids were closed there was no darkness! Anything but it! He was gazing into a colossal laboratory, or power-house, the size of which he had never even conceived or dreamt of. Figures, not entirely unearthly, but quite seven feet tall, were moving silently to and fro.

How crystal clear. How perfectly mirrored! As though he were actually present.

"Good God!" he exclaimed, sitting up startled, and looking round the bedroom to assure himself it was as it had ever been. "What on earth's happened to me?"

It was some time before he could recover from the shock—then, steeling himself, he lay down again and very falteringly closed his eyes once more. Instantly that vision returned, but enormous, though the temptation was, he did not reopen his eyes. He lay perfectly still, gazing into the brilliant picture mirrored in his mind.

Without the least effort he could see gigantic electric generators, bridged by triangular stairs of glittering metal, the apexes of these triangles being centered over engine-gangways. Then there were vast banks of levers and meters... He could hear nothing, but there hung about all that super-scientific immensity a suggestion of indescribable power; an awesome vision of intellect of superhuman quality, such as he had never thought possible in his entire scientific career, such as it had been.

Then presently something seemed to happen to him. He seemed to slide downwards very softly... Although he did not know it, he had fallen dead asleep.

That instant of breaking his contact with mundane things wrought an amazing change. For he was *in* the power-house. Not in the personage of Moore Holmes, but exactly in counterpart with his neighbors, almost earthly in body and head-development, yet of the remarkable height of seven feet six inches. Quietly he advanced to the nearest creature.

"Well, Zin, is everything progressing satisfactorily?" he enquired, and at that the other creature turned from examining a series of meters, and nodded. He was the possessor of a hard, cruel face and eyes that seemed curiously devoid of sentiment.

"Yes, everything, Master," he returned. "The etheric barrier is working perfectly. It will not be long before we shall be able to reduce earth's peoples to dust as the planet hurtles along in its orbit. Then we will have a pleasant world—a wonderful world—made so by the fools of Earthlings who have so long laboured to build and progress under our dictates. Amusing, is it not? And you, Laj? How are you progressing?"

"Perfectly," Laj answered calmly. "As the King-Lord, I have little to do but direct operations, but I concur with your views, Zin—the future is indeed full of prospect."

Zin smiled evilly. "You, as King-Lord, are to be envied—" he commenced—and at that juncture Moore Holmes awoke, to find himself on the bed just as he had been, dressed save for collar and tie. The electric light was still on.

Obviously he had slept—but whilst he had slept he had been somebody else! A totally different personality!

Apparently even another world altogether! That conception shook him considerably. He clambered from the bed and sorted out a small bottle of brandy from his locker. A stiff dose of the spirit brought some sane reason back to him.

"Etheric barrier?" he muttered. "King-Lord? Laj? Zin? What the devil…" He gazed at the ceiling contemplatively. "Yes, something's gone wrong with me since that damned lightning! That was no dream; I lived it! *Lived* it! I *was* Laj! Moore Holmes lost all entity for the time being. Good heavens! What a paradox of psychology!"

With another sudden effort he closed his eyes and found himself walking along a broad white roadway, lined on either side with graceful trees not unlike palms, in the light of a reddish-gold sun. The scene was reminiscently Egyptian, yet equally alien and unearthly. He came presently to facing another creature similar to the others, only less in height and more graceful of contour, attired in flowing robes of white.

No words could be heard, and it occurred to Moore that only during sleep could he hear anything. Otherwise his auditory nerves were keyed to earthly conditions. He opened his eyes again and once more sought the inspiring ceiling.

"A mental enigma," he said obviously enough. "I'm keeping exact time with that individual Laj. When I awoke just now, he must have walked out of the laboratory. I cut association with him. In that time, whilst I got off the bed he walked on to that roadway, and immediately when I closed my eyes I saw everything through his eyes once more! That creature must have been a female… Olania!

Good Lord, yes! *Olania!* I seem to remember something about that..."

The sudden realization that he was living the lives of two people came as a violent shock to the immature Moore Holmes. A glance at his watch assured him it was one o'clock in the small hours—an unpleasant hour, yet, despite it, he did not feel the desire to sleep any further. Indeed, the things he had witnessed and the crystal clear memories he had to dwell upon, had banished all thoughts of slumber from his mind.

"Yes, something has happened!" he declared with conviction, and sought in his mind to find scientific explanations, born of his own essentially meager training. He had no degrees to his name, was not even a B. Sc., but he did know the fundamentals of Einstein's theory and the supposed composition of a fourth dimension.

"Time is a function of that particular Space-Time Continuum in which we happen to find ourselves here and now, and Time doesn't extend to the fourth dimension. That is the belief of Professor Einstein," he said, to the gray oblong of night-filled window. "And yet, according to pure scientific reasoning, the subconscious in a human being's mind works *outside* the Space-Time Continuum. To the subconscious mind there is neither the barrier of space or time. Why? What the devil *is* subconscious, anyhow?"

The issue of that question was not altogether clear in the young man's mind—not at twenty three years of age, anyhow. He only knew something had happened defying all the normal laws of human make-up, and, that being so, he put back his collar and tie and digested the matter as he struggled with his stud. Every time he blinked he caught evanescent glimpses of strange buildings, complex cities, and once a desert of sand with mighty, flawlessly-straight waterways crisscrossing its burning vastness....

The mental phenomenon was not evaporating, then. He was still linked by some quite inexplicable mental force to that other life, which, before being struck by lightning, he had never even dreamt of.

Presently, redressed, he silently made his way through the dark silences of the sleeping college to the massive front door. In another moment he was outside in the Cloisters beneath the stillness of the stars. There was no moon, but the summer sky had the hazy translucence of light born of heat-mists.

Be it understood that Moore Holmes was no longer frightened—but he did feel that he could grapple with the mystery more satisfactorily out of doors. The cramping four walls of his bedroom lent an added terror to his strange mental adventures. Here, with only the horizon for limit, he could expand a trifle— But, when a man finds himself faced with the terrific problem of deciding the exact functions of the subconscious mind, he is faced at once with something baffling and profound.

And it was as Moore stood in silence, just outside the Cloisters, that he beheld away to the southern horizon something strange and, so far as he knew, unheard of. A mass of nebulous green light, perhaps as large as the moon, and quite distinctly visible. It might have been anything, something quite normal to the cosmos, had there not been attached to it an obvious ray of similar green, that stretched forth into infinity and was finally lost to sight.

Moore stared at it for a long time, then muttered to himself.

"Now what the deuce is that? It's not a nebula; it's being caused by that ray. And where does the ray go to? Hmmm, I don't seem able to follow it to the source; it's not being projected from earth, that is certain. From some other planet, perhaps…"

That jolted him. The recollection of the words he had heard—the words concerning an etheric barrier and the reduction of earth's peoples to dust… Something caught at his heart. Was that infernal haze an etheric barrier? It did not seem to grow any larger with the passage of minutes—and besides, where was it coming from? Thus was added another mystery to poor Moore's already overburdened mind. He couldn't tackle the problem alone, so not unnaturally his thoughts turned immediately to the one person who had any interest in him—Una Lanister.

Perhaps it was inconsiderate of him, but he turned on the spot and headed, *via* climbing the school gates, for the moor that led to her home, reached it some twenty minutes later, and hammered violently on the door of the little modern villa. Somewhere the guardian mastiff barked heavily in the night—then Una's father appeared, head and shoulders through the front bedroom window. Being a gentleman farmer of some repute he was more accustomed to giving orders than to taking them.

"Who is it?" he demanded petulantly, peering down at Holmes' dim, upturned face. "What the devil do you want at this ungodly hour?"

"It's me—Moore. Let me in, will you? I've something to tell you."

"Confounded foolery," James Lanister commented gruffly, withdrew his head gingerly, and presently opened the front door. He switched on the light and led the way into the front room, poising his massive figure on the edge of the sofa and regarding the young schoolmaster with duly mature suspicion.

"Well, Moore, what are you doing waking people up at this infernal hour?" he demanded. "You ought to be in bed, young man! I've no patience with this modern stuff!"

Moore was about to reply when Una herself, followed by her mother, entered the room, both with gowns hastily flung about them.

"Why, Moore, whatever is the matter?" Una asked quickly, running forward to him. "Aren't you feeling well? That lightning flash—"

"Oh, it's not that, Una. It's—something else. You see, I—er—I'm *two people!*"

"You're *what?*" demanded James Lanister blankly, standing up with the shock. "That—that isn't holy, young man. It is written that—"

"Be hanged what's written; I'm telling the truth," Moore retorted curtly. "Listen, Una;—perhaps you'll understand..." and he swiftly told her of his mental experiences, and his later beholding of the green nebula in the southern sky. "There's something weird about it all, Una—something different! And, if only I could get to the root-cause of my mental trouble, I feel sure something could be done. Believe it or not, the whole earth is in danger—danger from space, from other beings, who live on a planet full of deserts and big cities. Maybe Mars!"

"It is all terribly mysterious," Una agreed thoughtfully, stroking her chin. "You did right though, in coming to us. You're facing a big problem—"

"Perhaps you'd like a cup of tea?" Mrs. Lanister suggested, hugging her buxom form. "You look chilled, Moore—upset."

"Oh, there's no need to trouble, Mrs.—" Moore began, but the good woman was firm. She moved away, and stimulating hissings and spurtings from, the kitchen proclaimed her nocturnal endeavours. Mr. Lanister tapped his teeth unmusically; Una walked round in circles and continued to stroke her chin. Moore stood silent, his face perplexed.

"What about Doctor Mason at the college?" Una asked presently. "He said if anything went wrong with you, to see him again. He may be able to help you—"

"I never thought of him," Moore admitted. "He might be able to explain matters, but I doubt it. In a way, I'm half frightened of my condition. If I shut my eyes I see through the eyes of somebody else; if I go to sleep I am absorbed into the personality of that person—that creature Laj. And yet, I feel I must go on, for something is endangering the earth, and by pure chance I've stumbled on it. The lightning did it, that is clear, but—but what *is* the matter with me?" He looked helplessly round him.

"Indigestion," said James Lanister unimaginatively. "Now a good dose of—"

"You go and see the school doctor," affirmed Mrs. Lanister, who had just appeared with a steaming cup of tea. "Una's right. And if anything goes wrong, you can always rely on us to help you."

"Right enough," said Una warmly. "We'll stand by you, Moore."

"Fantastical rubbish!" said her father, pouting with impatience. "A nightmare! Huh! I've no patience with nightmares..."

"You've no patience with anything, James; that's what ails you!" his wife retorted curtly. "Keep quiet, or talk sense. It will puzzle you to do either, anyhow."

Moore sat down heavily, oblivious to the bickering—surrounded by perplexities, a girl with keen intelligence and some knowledge of science, and her unimaginative, faintly quarrelsome parents. He wondered, how any of them, even Una, could be expected to understand the laws of a Space-Time Continuum, a fourth dimension or a subconscious mind.

Still, the idea of consulting Doctor Mason was a good one. As he drank his tea, Moore decided he would act upon it....

CHAPTER II

After morning lessons the following day—lessons that were irksome to the troubled Moore Holmes—he called upon Doctor Mason, and was fortunate in finding him alone at the time.

"Oh, hello Moore!" The doctor's greeting was cordial. "Recovered all right from your lightning stroke? No headache or anything?"

Moore smiled mysteriously. "No—no headache. But, Doc, instead of developing such things as sixth sense, X-ray eyesight, clairvoyance, and other things attributable to being struck by lightning, I've got the most amazing malady of the lot. In brief, I am two different people. I'm a quiet Surrey; science-master on earth, and a King-Lord and master scientist on another world—probably Mars—at one and the same time."

That shook even Doctor Mason's habitual calm. He jumped from his swivel chair and advanced to where Moore was standing, his long face earnest and intent.

"You mean—you mean you're suffering from delusions?" he demanded keenly.

"Delusions nothing! I thought so at first, only I've substantiated it." Moore went on to explain his experiences and the discovery of the green nebula. "So, Doc, that unknown green nebula, and the ray reaching from it into infinity, proves indisputably that the etheric barrier, of which I heard, is not a figment. It *does* exist!"

"Ah, but even the nebula could have been a mental figment, Moore!" Mason remarked.

"It could—but it wasn't," Moore answered grimly, and with some difficulty withdrew a crumpled morning paper from his pocket. He handed it to the Doctor, motioning to a column rendered conspicuous with blue-pencil marks.

Mason commenced to read aloud.

"'Sir Arthur Langworthy, the noted authority on astronomy and psychology, who may be remembered for his discovery of the Triple-X-ray for investigation of brain troubles, announces that recent astronomical experiments he has conducted reveal the presence, some millions of miles from earth, of a strange and unknown species of atomic disruption. It would appear, he says, that this mass is actually a form of electrified ether, and could certainly arise by no normal celestial means. The attachment of a long ray to the mass leads Sir Arthur to think that creatures of another world, or existing somewhere in the cosmos, are deliberately causing the disturbance. Sir Arthur has not yet been able to determine if earth will ride into this mass during her orbital path, but if she does there is likely to be grave danger. His later findings will be published at the earliest moment'."

Mason ceased reading, his eyes showing that he was astounded. Moore smiled faintly.

"That's no delusion, Doc," he said quietly. "In that other life of mine, wherever it is, I'm actually the *cause* of this trouble. But I'm baffled as to know what to do. I can't analyse the subconscious; I haven't the knowledge or experience. I thought you might be able to help me."

Mason spread his hands helplessly. "My dear chap, I'm just a college physician and surgeon; I can't be expected to understand such matters as complex psychology. I know ordinary brain troubles and their remedies, but this is something different. It calls for an expert! Personally, I think the answer is in that newspaper. You ought to see Sir Arthur himself. He's a brain-specialist as well as an astronomer. I'll come along with you; your case is of absorbing interest to me,"

"But my work! I can't leave at a moment's notice! What is the Headmaster going to say?"

"Leave that to me," Mason answered purposefully. "I have decided that you need a change—have been working too hard. Your present mental condition demands the attention of a specialist, and I shall go with you to London. The Headmaster can't object to that. I'll fix everything, Moore, don't you worry."

"You're a good sort, Doc," Moore returned gratefully. "I can assure you that nobody will be happier than me to get this confounded trouble cleared up… I'll let Una know what's happening. She put me up to this in the first place."

It was nearly seven o'clock on the same day when Doctor Mason and Moore reached the Harley Street home of the celebrated Sir Arthur Langworthy. An appointment with him had, of course, been made over the telephone from the college, and a brief outline of Moore's astounding affliction had been more than enough to arouse the great man's curiosity…

Ushered into his private laboratory-surgery by an impassive manservant, Moore and Mason found the psychologist-astronomer puttering about amongst his scientific instruments, but he quickly came forward at their entry.

He was a man who immediately commanded interest—tall, massive-shouldered, with a remarkably lean face considering his build, lofty forehead, and a fringe of woolly, white hair around the upper portion of his cranium. His eyes, of a curiously violet shade, surveyed the two in an all-embracing glance.

"So here we have Mr. Holmes, the paradox of mental science?" he asked genially. "Well, well, how interesting! And you, Doctor Mason, suggested the problem might interest me? It does—most assuredly. But be seated, please… That's better! Now, Mr. Holmes, tell me everything."

Moore did so, to the smallest detail, and the expert listened in profound silence, wagging his head now and again and indulging in an occasional soft rubbing together of his skillful hands. When the story was over he stood for a long time with his active hands for once buried in the pockets of his velvet smoking-jacket.

"Amazing!" was his comment. "I begin to feel, Mr. Holmes, that your particular case is going to change all preconceived notions of science on what really constitutes a subconscious state of mind. You say that, in your other life, you distinctly heard the creature Zin imply that Earthlings were nought but the tools of the—er—shall we say, Martians?"

"Just that, sir," Moore assented.

"Clearly then, that proves the subconscious mind is not a haphazard thing—a line of consciousness entirely indeterminable—but something very real, that has been deliberately rendered mystifying that we may not know too much!"

"Good heavens, Sir Arthur, what on earth are you driving at?" Dr. Mason exclaimed. "Are you trying to prove the subconscious mind to be a—a myth?"

"Perhaps I am," the psychologist answered with a little chuckle. "You see, from normal standards the subconscious is explained rather unsatisfactorily. It is believed to be a region into which our experiences sink, and in which they continue to live an attenuated existence until the time when they are recalled into more complete life. Some scientists have likened it to the storeroom of memory, in which experiences are stocked, to be withdrawn when needed. At best this is distinctly unsatisfactory... Proof of the real power of the subconscious mind can be obtained from witnessing the efforts of an expert in clairvoyance or second-sight. Such people are born with more subconscious power than others—for reasons that may be clearer later.

"In your particular case, Mr, Holmes, being struck by lightning caused an unusual brain-transformation to take place. Namely, the region of the subconscious in your brain was suddenly rendered perfectly clear and understandable. And, do you know, I am just beginning to think that that region has been rendered enigmatical and impossible to probe *on purpose!* The strange chance that changed your mind into the state it is, has revealed for the first time what the subconscious really is! Namely, it is a region wherein we are actually attached to another life. Your own experiences alone prove that until you were struck by lightning, you had no conception of any life but your own. But, since then, you have found you can live as somebody else and live all his experiences as well. Briefly then, you have one mind divided between two bodies—each of you are a separate entity, but how the linking of mind comes about we have to still solve."

"But,' sir, they spoke English—referred to our world as earth, instead of some name of their own!" Moore protested.

"They only appeared to, my boy," the expert replied quietly. "You undoubtedly must have spoken the particular language peculiar to them, but when you remembered it in the ordinary way, it sounded like English, because it is the only language you know. You would assimilate their foreign language into your own in the waking state."

A silence fell at that—then Dr. Mason spoke.

"Sir Arthur, if this is true—this idea of a double entity as you theorize, might there not be other people on earth similarly affected?"

"If the theory I have in mind is correct, every human being on earth is so affected—every human being in the world is entirely at the dictates of another brain somewhere in the cosmos, presumably on Mars. Naturally, we do not know as yet how this miracle of mind-division has been accomplished, but we will try and find out, For the moment we can rest assured that the subconscious region in a man or woman's mind is really the region where he or she is actually another person—but, that other person has deliberately made the subconscious region dark and impenetrable, so that that other life can never be suspected or understood. A sheer accident—a flash of lightning—has broken that effect with Mr. Holmes, and he can see the other life quite clearly. Other people have developed tendencies to second-sight and similar gifts when struck by lightning—but none have had revealed to them the marvels Mr. Holmes has witnessed."

"Come to think of it, that would explain why we dream of places we've never seen, and in them meet people we've never known," Dr. Mason said reflectively. "Just hazy tracings of that other life, to which, if you're right, Sir Arthur, we belong."

"I do not imply we belong there—we are merely controlled from there," the expert amended. "This accident has happened very opportunely and links up with my later findings on the green nebula, as yet unpublished. In the space of roughly six weeks earth will hurtle straight into that maze. And, spectroscopic and electrical tests have revealed disconcerting facts, which fit in exactly with Mr. Holmes' conversation with the creature Zin."

"The doom of earth?" Moore asked grimly. "That's what you mean, isn't it?"

The psychologist's lean face became troubled. "Not of earth, my boy, but certainly of humanity. Just as humans will raise and fatten cattle, and then kill them off, so, in a different way, have these malignant beings seen fit, through unguessable centuries, to cause Earthlings to build up a perfect world, and then, when comparative perfection is attained, they will wipe Man out of existence. Yes, beyond doubt, the nebula is being controlled by intelligent beings. To explain what will happen, it will be necessary for me to turn to the field of astronomy and electricity… For instance, I need hardly state that Man is electrically constituted—built up of molecules and so forth, the basis of which is essentially electrical."

"Quite," said Moore, who knew that much by heart.

"Further, human beings are not composed of exactly the same electrical content as the earth itself—solid buildings, water, and so forth, because to a certain extent human electricity is always changing. State of health and outside influences can be cited as two instances... What I wish to impress is that humans are, fundamentally, electrical."

"Yes, but what—" Doctor Mason began, to be waved into silence.

"Now, what we call the inertia of matter, of human beings, is really attributable, of course, to the magnetic field of moving electric charges—inertia is electrical. It isn't due to something in matter itself, but to something surrounding it, and that something, more than probably, can be ascribed to the ether which the electric charge carries with it. Now here is the point. If electric charges are brought very close to each other they interfere with one another—the positive and negative tend to neutralize each other. So far as we know, it isn't possible to bring them into a complete coincidence in us, but these devils who exist in the cosmos *will* produce that effect in human beings! The etheric electricity they are generating, in the form of a gigantic electric power in the ether, will cause the entire obliteration of human beings, but not of earth, or buildings, or solids, because as I have already said, humans possess a different type of electricity."

"But—but how will humans be destroyed?" Moore demanded.

"I'm coming to it," Sir Arthur responded calmly. "Speaking from the standpoint of natural science, we know that electric charges can be brought very close to each other; hence their inertia is diminished. Two opposing charges at a distance apart will have double the inertia of one. If they are brought very close, the combined inertia will be less than double—indeed, some of their mass will disappear altogether—vanish out of existence. Hence, if actual coincidence is brought about, and these cosmic enemies of ours are seeing to that—it will mean the complete disappearance of every living thing. All human life, anyhow. Now do you see? I found all this out by telescopic and spectroscopic tests on the green nebula, and its effects on the ether in which it lies, but do not ask me to explain how these malignant scientists produce such effects. Their science is something beyond our ken—they control and destroy humans as we do insects. Minds like those will not be easy to fight!"

"To fight!" Moore echoed. "It seems to me they are untouchable!"

"No—not untouchable," Sir Arthur corrected quietly. "Thanks to your peculiar mind alteration, Mr. Holmes, it will be possible to get at these fiends and beat them at their own game. What we have to find out is where they are, how it comes about that they control the subconscious mind, and lastly find a means of stopping their activities. As yet, we are in the dark as to what they are driving at. If only we could find some way of viewing these creatures as clearly as you do! Let me think now…"

Sir Arthur turned and commenced to pace the laboratory slowly and pensively, chin on chest. Moore and Doctor Mason waited in strained silence.

"To reproduce my condition, sir, is impossible," Moore said presently, "The only thing we can do, so far as I can see, is for me to go to sleep, take on the entity of the creature Laj, and learn all I can. Steal information, as it were."

The scientist came to a halt. "Yes, maybe you're right," he agreed slowly. "At least, your suggestion will do for the time being until I can think further. You must stay here with me for a while, and Doctor Mason and I will watch over you whilst you sleep, on the off-chance that you may talk. Probably it will be in a strange language; but if not, we'll write down what we hear." He paused and considered. "I'm afraid you are going to find it a very weird experience," he added grimly.

Moore smiled faintly. "That doesn't matter much! After all, I'm a scientist, so I must get accustomed to scientific experiences. Suppose we start tonight—later on? You see, until I am actually asleep, I am not Laj: it is only when my own mind has ceased for a while to control my body that I become, as it were, part of him."

"Quite so," Sir Arthur nodded, "I will give you a sleeping draft that will make you sleep heavily—then maybe we'll learn something. In the meantime, since you are my guests, please come this way. We will have dinner—a trifle belatedly."

CHAPTER III

It was exactly eleven o'clock when Moore Holmes, fully clothed, lay down on the bed in the room Sir Arthur had had prepared for him. A sleeping draft rapidly brought the uncontrollable desire for slumber, and upon either side of the bed, anxious and intent, stood Doctor Mason and Sir Arthur himself, both armed with notebooks and pencils.

Moore himself instantly relapsed into that other "self" with which he had already become so cognizant—the "self" of the strange, seven-foot being known as Laj the King-Lord. He found himself in the great laboratory once more, the one he had seen the previous night, but now, owing to the brain influences of Moore, Laj was not entirely himself—not entirely governed by his own tremendous and ruthless brain.

Working by his side was the grim creature known as Zin.

"Six earthly weeks have but to pass, Master, then comes the extermination of the fools we have enslaved," Zin commented presently. "It has been our task to cause other beings to form for us a pleasant planet instead of this dying one of ours—and ere long we shall have succeeded."

Laj nodded slowly. "I wonder if all the other creatures of the cosmos prey upon each other, as we have done on Earthlings?" he murmured. "In a way it troubles me—this ruthless, cold-blooded control of an innocent race."

Zin was clearly astonished. "For twenty seven cycles you have been our Master—our King-Lord—and now, above all times, you are revealing that obsolete trait, known as sentiment, in your make-up. What is the matter, Master?"

Laj shrugged and rubbed his mighty forehead. "I cannot tell you, Zin. In some odd way I do not altogether feel myself. I am having difficulty in remembering things, too. Somewhere the perfect balance of my brain has been disturbed."

He turned away from the machine before which he had been standing and crossed to the massive window of the place. The view he absorbed was familiar—that of a stupendous city, block upon block, the topmost heights lost in the cloudless, green-blue sky. Infinities of glittering windows, the edifices connected and inter-connected by shining bridges of unthinkably tough metal.

On the ground level were the streets, orderly and precise, along which came and went swiftly designed machines; above the streets and below the bridges were the busy walking ways, crammed with seven-foot creatures, moving to and fro with certainty and purpose.

"The end of our world," Laj said at last, hands clasped behind him. "Six weeks for the earth to become suitable for us; seven weeks and our world dies. Atmosphere machines will have run their life; can no longer be renewed. The last scrap of water gone. Death—infinite and complete."

"Yes, but we will be in space heading for earth," Zin put in, coming up beside him. "Every living human will be dead, and you will be King-Lord of our new abode, unless anything arises to prevent it."

"Meaning what?" Laj asked coldly, with a half turn of his great head.

Zin spread his hands ingratiatingly. "Nothing, Master. But, even in our ordered lives there are sometimes—accidents."

"Only those you are likely to create!" Laj retorted. "You envy my position, Zin, I know, but do not attempt anything rash. If you do, you know the penalty."

Zin said nothing. His eyes merely seemed to glitter more brightly. In silence he joined his Master in silent speculation, until presently Laj aroused himself to speak again.

"I wonder why Earthlings have never suspected us," he murmured. "Probably because they cannot see or understand us clearly with their silly little telescopes. They have no means of understanding us, like we have them."

"No matter what they discover or what they do, they are compelled to be part of you and Olania," Zin answered grimly. "Do not forget that, from the very first instant that life began to spawn upon that world of earth, we—or rather you—hurled magnetism across the void, magnetism which contained a portion of your brain vibration known as will-power, and so forced the minds of those creatures to become subservient to your own—sending later a second destructive magnetism, which reacted upon their brains and so prevented them realizing that control was taking place."

"Very amusing!" said Laj laconically. "Earthlings, I understand, attribute everything inexplicable in their mental qualities to a subconscious region without explanation, but never realize for a single instant that on this world one man—myself—and one woman—Olania—perpetually keep the myriad masses of earth under control. It is concerning this control that worry has arisen, Zin. For some reason I find that, when I relax my will powers a trifle—an art we long ago cultivated, as you well know—I feel the presence of a somebody, an Earthling, who bears the preposterous name of Moore Holmes."

"Well?" Zin demanded, tight-lipped.

"I feel he may discover something," said the King-Lord gravely, still gazing out of the huge window.

"Needless worry," Zin commented curtly. "'How can such a thing be possible? In all the history of Earthlings not one has ever yet discovered that the subconscious is really a name for being controlled by another world—our world of Mars. How are Earthlings to even realize that their progressive inventions—radio, television, flying, and so forth, are all our own discoveries, which by *our* orders—or at least yours—they have similarly discovered, like children being taught by a parent. How in the name of the cosmos can one of them—this—er—Moore Holmes, for instance, possibly discover the truth?"

"I do not know, but it still worries me," Laj answered pensively; then alertly, as though banishing the thought from his mind, "Come—it is time for our inspection of the ether-magnetizing machines."

The two turned and, side by side, walked slowly through the wilderness of engines to a special section isolated in one corner. Here stood by far the most gigantic electrical engine in the whole place, thick cable wires linking up to a massive tube-like object, similar to a telescopic tube, securely imbedded in the ceiling of the place, the whole being set in universal mountings, so it could move in any direction.

Silently the two Martians surveyed the various dials with which the engine was supplied, and listened for a while to its steady humming—an unwavering hum that bespoke the incredibly perfect engineering of these brilliant and ruthless people. Both of them knew that into that tube-like apparatus was pouring, every second, ether-converting magnetism, which in turn was hurled into space in the form of a green ray, to create in ether itself, in the path of Earth's orbit, a mass of crushing electrical force, carefully calculated to be exactly in accord with the types of frequencies existing in human beings and all living things. It was inevitable, on entering that mass that every living thing on earth would perish. Everything inanimate would stand, ready for the Martians to take over.

Yes, the Martians had laid their plans very carefully and neatly, but even their tremendous range of intellect had not calculated that a stroke of earthly lightning could undo all their devices for sealing the brains of Earthlings. One Earthling, at least, about whom Laj had grave suspicions, was watching and living all this—indeed, performing all Laj's actions, hearing and understanding everything, whilst to outward appearances he was fast asleep....

"Yes, everything is in order," Zin remarked presently. "We have little to do but wait for the time to pass."

"For myself, I am minded to look again at those machines of mine which are responsible for the control of earthly brains," Laj answered. "I wish to reassure myself they are working properly. If anything were to happen now, it would ruin everything."

"But, Master, the machines have worked perfectly for countless cycles—both yours and Olania's!" Zin protested. "What is the matter with you, Laj? For a ruler you are behaving most strangely—queerly."

"It is not for the Under King-Lord to question his Superior," Laj returned with cold and withering dignity. "We will inspect the machines. Come!"

Silently, though his face was sullen, Zin followed his Master into the adjoining power-room, in the center of which, surrounded by guardian rails, reposed the complicated engines and varied mechanism that actually were responsible for that state of earthly mind known as "subconscious." The machinery, intricate though it was in appearance, was not too advanced in fundamental principle.

In the center of the machine, contained within a huge dome of indestructible metal, were two enormous electro-magnets. Upon these were indelibly impressed, by frequent renewals, the commands of Laj—thought vibrations. These vibrations, converted by massive and intricate transformers into electricity were passed in turn to transmitters, which were tuned to earth by the simple expedient of earth's own gravitational powers. It was inevitable then that the transformed vibrations of thought, when hurled through space, would go to the earth. Once there, by contact with the electrical nature of earth's upper atmosphere, the stratosphere, the vibrations were transformed back into their original state—that of thought-waves, and sought out the medium which would be of use to them—the brains of humans—just as a radio wave could only use a radio set in order to convert itself, and no other type of machine or instrument. The system was brilliant, beyond doubt, but so was the method of sealing human, brains afterwards to render them incapable of realizing that they were being controlled by anything but their own will.

From a machine annexed to the Brain Controller, the vibrations of which were guided to reach earth by a similar principle, issued forth a different type of electric energy, so high in wavelength as to be invisible, and being of the consistency of passing through the interstices of a human skull and into the brain itself, reacting upon that portion of the brain known as the subconscious—actually the Martian region, had Earthlings but known it...

What had happened to Moore Holmes was obvious, then. The lightning flash had created, in some strange way, a type of short-circuit, which had effectually earthed his brain from further disturbances by the Martian vibration for brain-sealing. He was no longer a conductor for this energy, but an effective insulation against it. Hence his brain, which since birth had been dominated by Laj, was able to perceive quite clearly the being who was responsible for his condition. Indeed, so strong was the force, that he *became* that person and lived in his mind the instant he cut himself off from external impressions by falling asleep.

It was manifest that Laj suspected something, somewhere—suspected that the brain of Moore Holmes was not altogether natural, but with all his ingenuity he could, find no way of getting to the root of the mystery. There was nothing to show, and even he could not dissect a thought and analyze it…

"I trust you are satisfied, Master?" Zin asked drily, after a space. "This examination, to my mind, has been to no purpose."

"When I am concerned with your mind I will mention the fact," Laj returned ironically. "For the moment we will say no more. I have work to do—work upon my secret machines."

"Why do you not reveal to the Council—to me—the nature of this secret work of yours? You owe it to us," Zin said bitterly.

"To you I owe nothing," was the King-Lord's response. "Leave me, Zin that I may work in private. You are too jealous of my power and position to be permitted to know everything."

"Laj, I warn you that—"

"You may go," returned the Martian ruler with frigid emphasis—and at that, with a bitter glance, Zin turned on his heel and stalked out of the colossal place…

* * * *

The entity of Laj passed slowly into gulfs of unknown mental reaches as Moore Holmes slowly awoke from sleep, to find two faces anxiously regarding him—Sir Arthur and Dr. Mason. They were strained faces, as though considerable effort had been exerted.

"A long vigil indeed," commented the psychologist at length. "You have been asleep five solid hours, Mr. Holmes. It is four in the morning now."

Slowly Moore rose into a sitting posture. "Five hours! But my experience lasted no more than thirty minutes—if that!"

Sir Arthur shrugged. "We cannot possibly determine the period of time taken in such a case as yours, where the effects are purely mental. The point we're concerned with is, did you see or hear anything of value? You spoke a lot, but in an unknown language. What happened to you?"

"I saw many things—heard wonderful things!" Moore breathed tensely. "You had both better listen carefully, while the memory is clear in my mind."

"Carry on!" Sir Arthur requested, and listened, as did Dr. Mason, in rapt attention as Moore proceeded. When it was over the elderly scientist slapped his leg emphatically.

"Upon my soul, that was worth waiting up for!" he exclaimed. "At last we know the cause of a subconscious mind, the meaning of the green nebula, and above all the fact that earth is indeed in danger. Now comes the point of deciding how to circumvent the menace."

Moore Holmes brooded over that. "I see no way," he confessed presently. "These Martian men are too clever for us."

"I wonder!" breathed Sir Arthur, rising from the bed and commencing his usual pacing up and down, rubbing his hands nervously the while. "I just wonder! This, for obvious reasons, cannot be an actual flesh-and-blood war, because we do not know how to cross space, mainly because you haven't stumbled on that secret during your mental experiences, Mr. Holmes. Obviating the physical possibilities then, that brings us to the mental."

"The mental!" Moore echoed derisively. "Good heavens, Sir Arthur, when will you realize that the beings we're up against are superhumanly clever? Against them dozens of our minds wouldn't match one of theirs! I know; I've been there."

"Exactly—you've been there," the scientist agreed, ceasing his pacing and coming back to the bed. "Why is it that you can see and do everything *via* Laj? Because a lightning flash earthed your brain against Martian resealing vibrations. You can see and live in the subconscious. You're the first man on earth to do it—but by heaven you'll not be the last!"

"Meaning what?" Dr. Mason asked, gazing at the psychologist's earnest face.

"Meaning that we've got to find out what portion of Mr. Holmes' brain was affected, and why! Then, duplicate the effect. By that process we'll be able to make any number of people see into the subconscious."

"Well, it sounds outlandish, but granting you could do it, where would be the benefit?" Mason persisted. "As I see it, from Mr. Holmes' experiences, Laj alone is responsible for the enslaving of earthly men—and this unknown creature Olania responsible for the women. If other earthly men were rendered capable of seeing into the subconscious, they too would only see via Laj, since his mentality is the supreme power back of it all. I can't see any benefit at all. Surely Moore alone is enough?"

"You miss the vital point, my friend," Sir Arthur responded intently. "We have the proof that the faint perturbations of Moore Holmes' will created in Laj a feeling of unsettlement; made him realize he was not altogether sanguine in mental outlook. His very actions showed he, for once, doubted his own abilities, much to the amazement of his colleague Zin. Doesn't it follow then, that the more minds there are trained upon him, the more disturbed he will become? The minds of say three men—Mr. Holmes, you, and myself, could so perturb Laj as to perhaps eventually, by mental suggestion, force him to destroy himself."

"My dear Sir Arthur, you underestimate Laj's mental powers!" Moore reiterated, thumping his fist on the eiderdown. "That creature controls all men with his own one mind, and then you suggest—"

"I disagree," the psychologist returned promptly, becoming heated. "He uses a high powered machine to amplify his thoughts—the one you saw yourself. That machine has impressed upon it Laj's normal thought vibrations, but those vibrations are increased in power enormously by electricity. Just as a person who has a record made of their voice can be heard, when the record is played, for perhaps a distance of a mile by amplifiers. The voice itself has not that power. Same with Laj; his mind alone is not capable of such enormous range and power; it is the mechanical intermediary that does the trick. I do not suppose for an instant that Laj's actual brain power is stronger than that of three combined human brains—if as strong."

"And what about Olania? She seems to control the feminine end," Mason remarked.

"For her, I was thinking of Miss Lanieter," Sir Arthur answered thoughtfully.

"You should tell your story to the world's greatest scientists," Moore commented sagely. "Never mind us— never mind Una—tell the brains of the world. Go for the thing in a big way. After all, it concerns all the world."

The scientist smiled bitterly. "I once made the mistake of telling the world of a great discovery and only just escaped being certified insane for the same reason," he replied reminiscently. "I shall tell nobody. Who would believe that the subconscious is really the region where we are controlled by a master-mind on the planet Mars? Not a single living soul—not even the cleverest… No, we'll keep it to ourselves. I do not quite know how Miss Lanister will react. She knows everything, of course, but—"

"Don't worry," Moore advised. "If you do succeed in reproducing my mental condition, I'll write her and get her to come along. She's sensible and intelligent enough to understand… Oh, and by the way, if we are controlled, how is it we also do things we like? That puzzles me not a little?"

"That is natural human will power—the very thing which is upsetting Laj's brain," Sir Arthur answered. "He can control, but he cannot usurp the priceless gift of each person's own individual will-power. That always remains."

"I see. Well, we can only hope that you will discover what happened to me…"

"We'll try tomorrow," the psychologist answered, stifling a yawn. "For the remainder of tonight Dr. Mason and I will try and get a little sleep. You, Mr. Holmes, do just as you choose. For you sleep is no sleep—just another waking existence."

"I'll just lie here and think things over," Moore replied, "You two go by all means; you must be tired…"

Sir Arthur and the doctor silently left the room and Moore, bedside light burning brightly by his side, studied the delicately carved ceiling over his head.

"Mars!" he muttered. "I begin to understand. They have manufactured their own air for unguessable ages, and now their machines are giving out. So they have had the earth made to suit their requirements by commanding Earthlings what to do. Amazing! That's what it is! Radio and kindred miracles of a modern age are nought but the dictates of Laj. I can't half believe it! And when his commands are withdrawn, if ever, what then? Will man not be able to progress? No—that cannot be. What is learned cannot be unlearned. Man will progress then by his own initiative, given a tremendous onward momentum by the science the Martians have imparted... That is *if* Laj can be destroyed..."

He ceased his soliloquy for a space, then, despite himself, he felt himself slipping back into a doze. Before he could make the necessary effort he was fast asleep again, breathing heavily... And, as before, Moore Holmes ceased to exist within himself.

CHAPTER IV

Laj the Martian, King-Lord of the stupendous scientific city to which he was devoted, moved slowly away from two complicated machines upon which he had been engaged, and presently gained the broad balcony that extended from his laboratory into the open air, at the highest point of the lofty edifice that was his palace, his machine rooms, and his home.

For a long time he stood looking down at the city in the light of the warm noonday sun. Once or twice he stroked his smooth, lofty forehead and muttered soundless words—then at a tap on his arm he turned, to find a lesser figure beside him—Olania.

Olania, the Martian woman, was perhaps six feet in height, having a few vague claims to earthly resemblance, being the possessor of a forehead as lofty as Laj's, and a pair of peculiar tawny-yellow eyes. In a fashion she was graceful, and moved with the consummate ease and dignity begotten of high birth and breeding, her long white robes, covering her from shoulders to ankles, flowing in the hot wind.

"So, Laj, you brood," she said presently, also gazing out over the city. "What is it that troubles the King-Lord? The Master?"

"Even a King-Lord can have his troubles, Olania," The Martian replied. "My mind is disturbed by unwanted influences—by the brain of one Moore Holmes, an Earthling. Nor, so far as I can see, is there any remedy. I am deeply baffled. I inspected the machine some time ago to be assured of their proper working. They are in order. I take it that yours are, too?"

The nearest approach to a laugh, came from Olania's massive, pendulous lips.

"Of course, Laj! You surely do not think that the minds of earthly women are left to chance? Oh, no! It amuses me, too, to think of your machine for controlling earthly men proving faulty. You—who are so clever!" There was cynicism in her voice.

"The machines are in order," Laj answered with dignity. "It is a brain, in a man called Moore Holmes that is causing all the trouble. If only one could get to grips with a thought…" Laj crushed a mighty fist on the stone rail before him in impotent silence.

"Perhaps, if your powers are weakening, you would like me to take over control of the males as well as the females?" Olania asked tauntingly. "I could—"

"Utterly absurd!" Laj snapped out. "You know as well as I do that no male mind can control female, or *vice versa,* because both have their individual characteristics. That is why when males and females first appeared on earth, my gracious sire allotted me the task of controlling males, and you females—because we are to be mated. Let there be no more talk of you taking over control. I have never failed, and never shall—but the personality of Moore Holmes, and his will power, are to me like a grain of sand in a smooth running mechanism. There is infinitesimal friction, and if it increases, that friction can destroy the whole machine... I am deeply troubled!"

"And how have you spent your time? Trying to solve the problem?" Olania asked very quietly,

"No; I have merely been busy on my two secret machines, the details of which you yourself know. Never reveal anything about those machines to Zin, Olania. He is jealous of my power; you know that."

"So am I," she returned, her face hardening. "You, the King-Lord, calmly spend the morning with your two secret machines, just to flatter your vanity, and don't try and find out what's wrong with your own brain! Remember, Laj, that unless you reveal yourself as you have always been—master of yourself and your brain—you are no longer entitled to be King-Lord."

"Meaning what?" Laj asked in a low voice.

"It should be clear enough. We are to be mated—the Council has determined that... When that happens I shall become the Queen-Mistress. But, doesn't it occur to you that to be the ruler of my peoples, without being your mate, might have greater advantages?"

"But, Olania, we have respect—even love—for each other!"

"Love! That died aeons ago! Power is the greater mo-
tivator in our lives, Laj. In my control of earth's females
I have never made a blunder, and I never shall. You, the
King-Lord, actually admit that you *have* made a blunder.
That, by our scientific reasoning, makes you unfit to hold
power. Your removal from power will mean my installa-
tion, since we are prospective mates. You know the law
of the city, of our planet, Laj. You have broken what we
know as the Rule of Infallibility, in which no man may
retrogress or reveal mental disturbance—or woman either. You admit you are mentally upset."

Laj's massive lips compressed. "And what regard
you had for me—that regard of which you have so often
spoken—means nothing, then?" he asked grimly. "You
would betray me because of a baffling mental weakness,
to the Council of Judicature, and so take my place?"

Olania shrugged. "Regard has no place in the minds
of true scientists," she answered coldly. "I would do just
as you have said, and place Zin in your stead, under my
control, to rule earthly males. Not that that will be really
necessary, for by that time we would have started the mi-
gration to earth. It is just as well you realize what powers
I have got, Laj. I am no fool."

Laj became silent at that, for a space. Then,

"So you would betray me; you in whom I trusted; to
whom I told the secret of my two special inventions; with
whom I hoped to share my life and triumphs on earth
when we arrive to take over possession. Science has
killed all your sentiment, Olania."

Olania's face revealed a faint sign of puzzlement at
that. "Zin has already mentioned to me that you have revealed sentiment today. You are doing it again now. What
is the matter with you, Laj? Before this mental disturbance

you were the ideal Master—as cold and faultlessly balanced as the machines you control, and as impartial as infinity itself. *I* am no different; it is *you*!"

"I find it there; I can do nought but admit it," was Laj's slow reply. "It is, I agree, an element long dead, but evidently it was only dormant. I must find means to check it..."

Olania drew her fluttering garments about her at that, tossed another glance at the colossal city, and then looked back at the silent ruler.

"I will give you until tonight to come to your senses, to master your own will and rid yourself of the influences of this ignoramus you call Moore Holmes. Above all, you must banish that archaic element known as sentiment! If you do not do so, I shall place the entire matter before the Council of Judicature. Goodbye."

She paused on that note and looked again at Laj's set and powerful profile against the blue of the cloudless sky. "You know, Laj, even a woman can love power," she added in a softer voice. "Laj or otherwise, regard or matehood, nothing could suit me better than to be sole ruler... That is all."

"I have heard," Laj answered in a somber voice, and never removed his gaze from the embodiment of power that was the city.

Perplexities! Disturbances! Something interrupting the usually smooth-running currents of his tremendous intellectual stream. Moore Holmes! *Moore Holmes!* The fierce, insistent, individual will-power of the innocent Surrey schoolmaster grew with the passing hours upon his consciousness, so delicately was the Martian brain adjusted. The slightest untoward influence could mar that supreme alignment.

Moore Holmes... Somewhere, something was amiss...

* * * *

It was full daylight when Moore awoke, the bedside light still burning by his side. To his surprise he found that, although he had lived as Laj, his body was refreshed as though with natural sleep. He decided it was a clear evidence of detachment of mental from physical power.

Over breakfast he made the outline of his later experiences clear to Sir Arthur and Doctor Mason.

"So we approach a little nearer!" Sir Arthur exulted, tackling eggs and bacon with most unscientific detachment. "The creature Olania, of whom we have heard but little until now, is the controller of female brains, and Laj of the male. We have that quite clear now. And will there be some fireworks when Olania discovers that the same thing that has been upsetting Laj is also upsetting her!"

"One fact is obvious," Doctor Mason said, in the manner of one who has arrived at a momentous decision. "Laj will not be able to break the influence of Moore, or will he overcome sentiment, because it is a part of Moore's own mind. That means Olania will head for the Queenship, or whatever they call it, and Laj will be deposed. What then? Granting your experiments succeed, and Miss Lanister is agreeable to helping us, how can she influence Olania?"

"If what Olania said is true, she will not be the Queen-Mistress until after the end of the earthly race—and that won't be much good!" Moore grunted.

Sir Arthur smiled tolerantly. "My dear chap, if we succeed, Miss Lanister's influence over Olania will make her as incapable of ruling as Laj himself—then where will the pair of them be? They are, obviously, the controllers of

Mar's destiny, outside of their infernal Council of Judicature, and so if both of them develop the same faults they will keep quiet. That will mean that Laj will continue as undisputed ruler. All this, of course, granting that Miss Lanister's mental powers are sufficient to upset the balance of Olania's brain. If not, we shall have to let other women into the secret, but not if we can avoid it. We know that these mental disturbances are progressive in action. At first, Laj was not much disturbed by Moore's mental efforts, but as the time has passed the intensity of the trouble has increased. If we can add two more minds to Moore's—my own and yours, Doctor Mason—Laj will not know what the devil he *is* doing. We can try and make him withdraw that etheric barrier."

"And Olania?" Moore asked quietly.

"Well, granting Miss Lanister is up to it, we can make Olania agree with Laj in his ideas. That will mean that the two principal beings on Mars have ordered the withdrawal of earth's destruction, and because those two *are* the virtual rulers of Mars nobody else can disagree. It's all perfectly simple."

"Zin will have something to say about that; so will the Council," Moore commented grimly.

The psychologist shrugged. "Probably so. Still, we have a scheme to work on, anyhow. The first thing to do is to try and duplicate Moore's strange mental powers…"

So, when the breakfast was concluded, Sir Arthur led the way into the laboratory and locked the door, changing, as though with a wave of a wand, into the alert, penetrating scientist that the world knew—the wizard of psychology.

"I imagine we can get to the source of the region of the brain affected by the use of my Triple-X ray," he said, once more rubbing his hands. "You have heard of it from the newspapers, no doubt… Here it is."

He led the way to a machine resembling a television receiver at the far end of the room. The main feature of the apparatus was a screen of some dark substance, and numerous wires and terminals were around the screen's edges, the wires themselves leading back to a helmet adorned with plugs and adaptors of varying shapes and sizes.

"You see, one dons the helmet, and by doing that the various frequencies from those adaptors cause a vibratory impression of the brain itself to be received, which are enormously magnified and passed on to this screen. The result is a much enlarged picture of the brain. And here is the virtue of my invention. Any part of the brain which is not absolutely normal is shown as black, because the least fault in the vibration causes a short circuit which immediately puts out the current of the wire leading from that particular spot. So, we may get to the cause of Mr. Holmes' trouble, find its situation, and then endeavour to produce the same effects. Now, Moore, if you will sit in the chair, we'll try and find something out."

Moore nodded, seated himself, and permitted the scientist to fasten the helmet on his head, securing it with a strap beneath his chin.

"So far, so good," Sir Arthur murmured, and turning to the control board he threw on the power, watching the red safety bulb that immediately came into life, and then glancing at the three electro meters which gave the voltage reading. Satisfied at length, he joined Dr. Mason in watching the screen, which, despite the daylight, was; already suffusing with a brilliant silver light… Slowly, gradually, out of the bars of silver and mist, there began to appear a gigantic, mirrored picture of the brain of Moore Holmes.

The whole business was scientific brain surgery of a remarkably high order.

Presently the picture was clear in all its details from the cerebellum at the base, to the summit of the fissure of Rolando at the top. For a while it seemed that the brain was perfect, then Mason and Sir Arthur started I forward eagerly as they beheld a slowly appearing black patch, which quite abruptly, as the circuit was cut off, came into sharp relief. It lay to the right of the frontal lobe, nearly touching Rolando's fissure itself.

"So, that is the affected spot!" Sir Arthur breathed. "Excellent—truly excellent! By some vagary of electricity that was the portion of Mr. Holmes' brain that was affected, and which opened the subconscious region to his knowledge. I will take a photograph of it at once."

He brought a heavy camera into operation, took several photographs to be assured of at least one clear result, then switched off the Triple-X Ray. Moore took off the helmet and got to his feet at the scientist's behest.

"So you found it, eh?" he asked, for he had seen everything.

Sir Arthur nodded. "Yes. Once these plates are developed we'll know exactly how we stand. Pardon me a moment whilst I go into my darkroom."

He went off eagerly to an enclosed portion of the laboratory, to return perhaps fifteen minutes later with four dripping prints in his hand. Three were not too good, but the fourth was a masterpiece. Moore's whole brain was clearly in evidence, with the dark spot wherein, literally, lay the key to another world!

"Now what?" Mason asked. "Reproducing lightning is going to be ticklish, isn't it? You might kill us trying that out."

"On the contrary, my dear Doctor, if I thought that, I would think it clear that I should go no further. It seems to me that the electrical shock, which Mr. Holmes received was only the minutest portion of the full power of the lightning flash. It *must* have been. Had he received the full force, he would have been blasted into powder. It reached him, we find, by way of his left arm. That so, Moore?"

The young science-master nodded, pushing up his sleeve to reveal his still bandaged forearm.

"It seems logical to assume then that the connections by nerves from the arm to the brain will bring us exactly to that spot which was affected in Mr. Holmes," the expert went on eagerly. "You understand? Of course, every part of the body is connected by nerves to the brain, but it is not altogether easy to determine where the nerve-endings come.

"In Moore's case, we have absolute proof that the connection to the subconscious region lies entirely in the forearm nerves, maybe deep below the surface skin. This photographic print shows the brain connection clearly. I propose, as an experiment, to use ordinary electricity, which is lightning in modification, of course, and apply it to my own arm, in exactly the same position as that elongated blister on Mr. Holmes'. You will have to take the bandages off for that, Moore. Then, as the power is increased, I can determine if the same effects can be reproduced."

"How much voltage?" asked Dr. Mason uneasily.

"Oh—er—start with twelve and work up. I can stand that."

"You've got a nerve, sir," Moore commented candidly. "The shock I got knocked me silly for the time being. I might have been killed, even. Twelve volts won't do any good. It was more like 4000 that hit me!"

Sir Arthur shook his head. "Couldn't have been; you'd have been killed stone dead. However, I think I know enough to stop before I go too far. Besides, we have little option but to go ahead if we want to try and save the world. You can assist me in constructing a gadget for the experiment."

He moved to his electrical bench, and the morning passed in the construction of an instrument somewhat resembling one for testing blood-pressure. To a long strip of copper foiling, interspersed with rubber bindings to render the thing elastic, were soldered eight copper wires, all leading back to a small generator, which was capable of controlling electric voltage from as low as 10 volts to 1,000 by specially made regulators. The result would be that the current would pass into the copper foiling and thereafter into the nerves of the arm, thence to the brain.

What the result would be the experimenters did not then wish to conjecture.

Sir Arthur seemed satisfied enough; he ate a hearty dinner, despite what lay before him, then, after a large-sized cigar and a brief chat he led the way back to the laboratory and lay down on the table that had been prepared for the purpose, possessing rubber matting on the top next the body, and a rubber insulated earth-rod to be gripped by the hand of his disengaged right arm. This would at least provide some insulation for the body.

"Carry on," the scientist said grimly, and, assisted by Mason and Moore, slid the armband into position. This done he lay down at full length and cocked his head to watch the voltmeter readings from the generator.

"Right!" he ordered, and gripped the earth-rod.

For a moment Mason, who was operating the resistances, hesitated—then, shrugging his shoulders fatalistically, switched on the power at 10 volts.

"Increase," said Sir Arthur after a while. "I can't even feel that!"

So the power was allowed to become stronger until presently it reached 25 volts.

"Good—my arm is tingling!" the psychologist remarked in satisfaction. "Proceed—higher! Higher, man!"

The power moved up to 50…75… The expert gripped the earth-rod with a vice-like clasp. His jaw was set and immovable.

"More!" he ground out presently.

"But, Sir Arthur, it's electrocution—" Mason protested.

"Shut up! *More!*" Sir Arthur almost snarled, and the power leapt up to 100 volts. His arm began to tremble apparently of its own accord under the increase. Perspiration broke out on his face with the tremendous strain.

"Not enough. More yet!" he panted.

Dr. Mason again obeyed and marvelled how the old man stood it as the power rose higher and higher, volt upon volt—until presently the 180 mark was reached. At this, Sir Arthur suddenly relaxed and became still. Instantly Mason cut the machine off.

"He's—he's dead!" Moore shouted in horror.

"No, he isn't," Mason returned curtly. "Just passed out, that's all. No wonder! Give me a hand, will you…"

Between them they lifted the scientist from the table and placed him in a nearby chair. Under the influence of *sal volatile* and cold water, he began to recover consciousness. At last his eyes opened, and after a long pause he spoke.

"It worked!" he breathed. "180 volts is the number. Just at that instant I caught a glimpse of a stupendous city, such as Moore described—then, when I lost consciousness, I took on the form of Laj, entirely as we anticipated. Yes indeed"—he closed his eyes for a moment—"it is successful. I see through the eyes of Laj when I close my own. We have succeeded! Except for a headache and a blistered arm I'm none the worse. If we took the trouble to use my Triple-X Ray, I'll warrant we'd find my brain black in the same spot as Mr. Holmes'…"

He peeled the armband off and revealed a red, burned arm.

"It's a hellish process, savoring of mediaeval torture, but there is no other way," he said grimly. "Ointment will soothe this. The point is, Doctor Mason, are you willing to undergo the same thing?"

"Certainly," the doctor assented readily. "I'm no weakling. The only thing I am really worrying about is—"

"I know—Una," Moore remarked. "You needn't—either of you. She is a woman of courage; she'll stand it."

The psychologist shook his head slowly. "I don't like asking any girl to subject herself to such merciless treatment," he muttered. "It's—it's devilish. Suppose she couldn't stand it? Suppose we killed her?"

"In a case of this sort, it is for her to decide," Moore replied quietly. "I'll wire her to come right away, then we can make up our minds. She'll be here by evening if I telegraph right away."

Sir Arthur nodded. "Very well, you do that. Whilst you're about it, I'll fix Doctor Mason up with the process. Now, if you are ready, Doctor?"

"Entirely," Mason assented, without hesitation, lying down on the table—and so, operating the current himself since Moore had left for the post-office, Sir Arthur got to work on the school doctor's arm.

He too passed into a faint in the concluding moments, but recovered shortly afterwards, to find the work had been successful. He, too, had been admitted to the subconscious region...

So were born two more personalities to further upset the equilibrium of the brain of the super-being, Laj the Martian...

CHAPTER V

At eight o'clock that evening in response to Moore's telegram, Una presented herself, baggage and taxi, at the scientist's residence. A housekeeper, with more interest in cooking than in the world, directed her to her room— then, after a late meal, Sir Arthur outlined the whole scheme of things to her.

His narration left the girl in a thoughtful mood.

"Well," she said presently, "you men have discovered wonderful things and done wonderful things, but in my opinion you have made a huge mistake in regard to the opinion you have of Laj and Olania."

"In what way?" Moore demanded. "They're both nothing more than a couple of cutthroat, ambitious devils. Don't you realize, Una, that for centuries—ever since our human race began—these two creatures have controlled earthly men and women, purely for their own ends? Have literally done what they like with male and female brains."

"I know it," the girl nodded quietly. "Now they are trying to wipe out every human being, which you men interpret as a fiendish thing to do. But you have forgotten to include that in their doing that lies a necessity. Their world is dying. They must find another abode, so, not unnaturally, they choose the abode they have prepared, much as we would prepare a house and go into it."

"We wouldn't kill the occupants, to get into it," Dr. Mason pointed out.

"If you were faced with death as the alternative, you would," the girl returned with calm firmness. "You men have made a mistake in considering these Martians to be a ruthless and terrible people. Immediately you decided you would try and get the man Laj to kill himself. In that you also are murderers! You are, quite unconsciously, revealing the same strain that causes wars on earth. No woman ever started a war, gentlemen—men alone do that. And will do—because they have more of the beast in them than a woman has."

Sir Arthur rubbed his hands together in delight.

"Excellent, Miss Lanister! You are a really remarkable young lady! Upon my soul, I would never have suspected a young woman of your age would take so much interest in our work. Please go on."

"It seems to me, that if these Martians are as terrible as you imagine, they would have come to earth before now to achieve mighty conquests. They can cross space; you have found that out. Yet they never have done so. Until absolute necessity has arisen they've left us alone, but have controlled our minds to make this planet fit for them when they need it. That alone points not to wilful extermination, but to dire need."

Moore grunted. "What do you propose we do then? Drop the whole thing? Let humanity be destroyed by the green nebula?"

"Anything but it," Una answered slowly. "I am quite willing to undergo the brief pain necessary in order to become admitted to the mind of Olania, my subconscious mind, but I make one stipulation."

"Yes?" Sir Arthur's eyebrows elevated enquiringly.

"That I handle Olania in my own way, as I see best in my own judgment. You men do as you wish."

"Fair enough," Moore answered. "Are you sure you can stand the electric current, though? It might—kill you."

The girl smiled faintly. "It'll take more than that to kill me. All I want to know is, when do we start? The sooner the better, you know."

"Well, you are tired after your journey today. Suppose we say tomorrow?" Sir Arthur suggested.

"And lose a night?" the girl exclaimed. "Foolish policy, Sir Arthur. Why, when I sleep tonight I may just as well sleep to some purpose, instead of dreaming a lot of silly, irrelevant rubbish. Better 'electrify' me right away, then when I go to bed I can get busy on Olania."

"Well, if you insist…" The psychologist shrugged.

"Certainly I do! Come along—let's get it over with."

Una rose purposefully to her feet; the men glanced at each other in silent amazement and admiration, then Sir Arthur preceded them to the laboratory. So for Una, as it had for Doctor Mason and Sir Arthur, the electricity got to work via her left arm to her brain. With amazing courage and strength she clung grimly to full consciousness up to 120 volts, then the pace was too much for her and she swooned.

With cold persistency, the psychologist increased the voltage to the requisite 180, watching her limp arm jumping visibly with the current. Once that mark was reached he switched off and the girl was swept off the table, immediate measures for her resuscitation being taken.

* * * *

In ten minutes she had recovered again, to find her arm wrapped in ointment-smeared bandages. That faint, courageous smile flitted over her features.

"All right, Sir Arthur, what are you worrying about?" she asked at last. "It was worth it, wasn't it? I've already seen through Olania's eyes, and because I am also a woman I can see something of her viewpoint in desiring power over Laj." She straightened up from her huddled position. "I propose that when we retire tonight we strain every mental concept to bring matters to a head," she said quietly. "We might as well do it now as later. Is it agreed?"

"If you are up to it, yes," the psychologist agreed.

Una nodded. "All right, then. If you've no objection I'll retire right away. My head is aching, just as yours did. It'll pass off… Now, don't forget! Work with might and main!"

"We will," Moore assured her. "Shall I help you to your room?"

"Good heavens, no!" She rose to her feet, holding her bandaged arm. "I'll manage all right—trust me." And with that she turned and slowly left the laboratory.

The three men glanced at each other.

"Now that is what I call a woman," Sir Arthur breathed admiringly. "Courage and resource, and yet—femininity. Moore, my boy, you are a fortunate young man."

"Yes, I suppose I am," he admitted. "We'll do as she says, too, and concentrate for all we're worth tonight. Suppose we get to bed right away and have a long night? Eh?"

"An excellent suggestion," Sir Arthur agreed. "Come—let us go."

* * * *

Laj the Martian walked slowly along the aisle between the machines of which he was the master, and presently gained his usual position on the balcony overlooking the city. It lay before him, white and immense in floodlights, for the Martian night had arrived.

For quite some time he stood watching the satellite Deimos on its leisurely path through the heavens, then his gaze swung to the western horizon as the satellite Phobos suddenly appeared—active little Phobos, swinging round Mars in slightly over seven and a half earthly hours. Phobos, who always rose in the west... Then presently Laj's eyes wandered away from the scurrying satellite to a bright green star low down on the horizon—earth. The nearest approach to a smile seemed to touch his heavy lips.

"The new life—the new being of our race," he muttered. "It has been worth it, and yet..." He fell to silence again, eyes brooding now on the city's egregious mass—then they moved on to the gleaming ribbons of the dying waterways. "A pity that such mental upset should disturb my progress at this point," he murmured presently to the thinning air. "Far from improving, my mental troubles have increased. I see now three personalities, where formerly there was only one. This is indeed serious."

"Is it?" inquired a voice, and a half turn assured him that it was Olania moving very slowly towards him. Silently he realized it was time for her to arrive for her decision.

"So, Olania, you have come to betray me to the Council," he commented quietly—then turned to look directly at her as she remained silent. He beheld her outlined against the brilliance of the laboratory behind her; his eyes caught the reflected light from a massive machine facing the balcony—one of his secret machines.

"I wonder if I *have* come to betray you," Olania muttered at last.

"What do you mean by that?" Laj spoke with the imperiousness of the ruler he was.

"I mean that I too have fallen a victim to mental disturbances, Laj! You are not alone; we are both in the same position. You perhaps more than I—but there it is! I cannot betray you, for you can betray me, and between us we should lose control. That would mean the downfall of our race, for we are the foundations on which it is built."

"Very true," said Laj solemnly; then after a pause. "I have been wondering these past few hours why it is that progress and power must always be at the expense of something lesser. Somebody with feelings, like us, has to be destroyed in order that we, the masters, may stride over it all."

"Sentiment again," Olania murmured. "I derided you this morning, Laj, for that queer emotion, only to find tonight that I have it myself. I can dimly see the formation of an earth woman in my mind—a Una Lanister."

"I see as many as three earth men," Laj responded grimly.

"Then it means only one thing," the Martian woman decided. "The creatures whom we have controlled for all these cycles are at last becoming cleverer than us! They have found out our secret, Laj, and their minds are disturbing ours. That is inevitable after the centuries and ages that have passed during which human minds have been linked to ours. They will seek a vengeance, Laj. Suppose a hundred men tackle you, and a hundred women me. They could upset our delicately adjusted brains so much as to drive us to insanity!"

Laj frowned. "That doesn't seem to be their object, Olania. All they have done is to bring an element of sentiment to worry along with."

"The woman Una is doing more than that to me," Olania said. "I feel, I even see—differently. I begin to realize, either through her brain or my own, that all this is a terrific mistake. We have made progress and lost sentiment, and sentiment, Laj, although I ridiculed it earlier today, is the foundation of true life. We had it once, and lost it in this mad, ridiculous maze called—science!"

"So I feel, too," Laj said in a low voice. "Before today I looked with pleasure on traveling to that glorious world of earth—on seeing our race progress in a world made for us by fools who do not understand their own brains. But, since the arrival of these disturbing mind-influences, I have thought differently. In some way—I am changed! Perhaps I am a fool!'

Olania shook her head. "You are thinking that the destruction of one race that another—ours—might live, is unjust?" she asked softly. "You feel that you are striding too far? Usurping?"

"Just that...." Laj confessed, and then relapsed into momentary silence.

Olania shrugged her shoulders and looked towards the sinking green dot of earth.

"After all, *can* we progress much further?" she asked quietly. "There is a limit, even to progress. We have mastered all the sciences; there is little more to really accomplish, except for going on living, amidst the luxury of what we have achieved. We shall not actually go any further. Like being born again, but with all our knowledge there to start with. The same old things—always. And upon our consciences there will always lie the indelible memory—we destroyed that *we* might live!"

Laj considered through an interval. "Our world will die in a few weeks—so will earth's peoples. We are facing a gigantic question Olania. Which shall die? Earth, or Mars?"

The silence of profound thought descended upon that problem. On the earth, three men and one woman, fast asleep, strained every atom of their alert subconscious minds to influence the sensitive brains of the 40,000,000 mile distant Martians on the laboratory balcony.

At last Laj spoke in his profound voice.

"It is better that we admit our progress has ended—that our race has run its course and must die there. Progress further we cannot; we can only live in what we have already attained. What right have we to destroy a world's peoples? None! For you and me, Olania, there can always be the eternal sleep, beneath the eternal stars. Not material matehood—no King-Lord and Queen-Mistress—but the interweaving of our respective great minds. Together, with the knowledge we possess, we can wing eternity and sweep, unhampered, to the furthest star."

"How true," Olania murmured, moving closer to him. "Until now cold science has held us apart; we have to thank the Earthlings for bringing us back that forgotten element—love. To admit the end has come is befitting of a mighty race."

"So be it, then," Laj said, standing erect. "I, the King-Lord, have proclaimed it! Our world shall die! Earth shall be freed! Tomorrow, I will inform our peoples; they cannot defy my edict. Tonight I will stop the etheric barrier machine and remove the danger to earth's peoples. After that—comes the end."

"A rightful end—" Olania began, then stopped and looked round in alarm as a figure darted swiftly forward on to the balcony, face contorted with rage, It was Zin.

"What is this utter foolery I have been overhearing?" he demanded savagely, glaring at the two in turn. "Save earth! Let Mars die! Laj, have you taken leave of your senses?"

"How came it you dare to overhear? Further, how dare you question my edict?"

"When it involves my life, and the life of our race, I dare question anything!" Zin retorted. "For too long now you have been secretive and mysterious. Those two secret machines of yours, for instance. Your recent leaning toward sentiment… And now, this! You are going to plunge every living soul on our world into death. Let us die in the cold and airlessness of the void itself."

"You heard me say our race has run its course," Laj returned steadily. "Do not dare to disobey me, Zin, or it will be the worse for you—"

"Both of you are being influenced by minds other than your own!" the Martian spat out venomously. "But we shall see if you can destroy our people as easily as that!

It was only my suspicions of you that led me to listen to your conversation with Olania tonight, and now I have found you out. You traitor!"

"Zin, how dare you—" Laj began furiously, then before he could proceed any further the inflamed Zin had flung himself forward. In a moment he bore the King-Lord to the stone floor.

Desperately the two Martians staggered back and forth along the balcony. Laj was a powerful creature, but so was Zin. The trouble was that Zin was aided by an all-consuming fury that lent triple strength to his powerful muscles.

The encounter was very brief—and tragic.

Seizing a momentary opportunity, Zin seized his master round the waist and lifted him high in the air to the balcony rail. Laj struggled desperately, but a blow in the face half-stunned him for a moment. The next instant he was flying out into the darkness—down towards the stupendous city below. Down to instant death...

Olania stood stupefied, paralyzed. The mind of Una swung her over to grief and tears, and for the first time in her unguessably long life, moisture welled up in her eyes. Through the blur she saw Zin, grinning devilishly, approaching her....

* * * *

Back on earth, at the identical moment of Zin's approach towards Olania, three men and a woman simultaneously awoke. Within five minutes they had sought each other out and, hastily attired, went down into the lounge.

Sir Arthur switched on the lights and handed brandy round with grim solemnity.

"We are faced with a crisis," he said quietly. "Since we all beheld the same thing, we know exactly what took place. When one of us awoke, we all awoke, by a subconscious union of thought. We all know that, for menfolk at least, the power of the subconscious control is forever broken. Laj, Master of Mars, is dead."

"And if Zin has his way, Olania will soon follow suit," commented Mason gravely.

"Exactly so." Sir Arthur stood silently considering for a moment. "As far as we men are concerned, our power is ended. We can no longer view Mars or its inhabitants, because the link snapped when Laj died. His machines alone are useless, because they have not the power to *think.* The issue is left, therefore, with—Olania."

"With me, you mean," Una remarked, setting down her glass. "Upon my shoulders rests the incumbency of trying to save a world."

"It is not right that you alone should face it," Sir Arthur exclaimed. "Let us get other women to help you. Alone, you don't stand a chance!"

"You think not?" Una asked. "You saw for yourself how, single-handed, I swayed Olania over to sentiment, whereas it took three of you men to sway Laj. Do you know why? Because Olania is a woman, being tackled by a woman, and in, that very fact lies her undoing. She would be more than a match for any army of men with her subtleties, but a woman, embodying the same subtleties as herself, playing craft with craft, mind against mind, can overcome her single-handed. And the main reason for my control over her is that I have swayed her towards *sentiment,* and inborn in every woman—I care not what planet she belongs to—is that one irrestible element... Laj was a harder case. It took three men to win him over.

I alone, I remain convinced, can master Olania and save the earth. In any case, there is not the time to call in other women and explain everything to them."

The psychologist shrugged his shoulders. "Very well then, Miss Lanister. Since you seem so confident, you had better resume activities right away. If you will sit in that chair I will give you a sleeping-draft. There is no time to lose."

The girl nodded calmly and sat down, Mason and Moore on either side of her, regretful that they could not view through the Martian eyes of Laj any longer. Sir Arthur disappeared into his laboratory, to presently return with the sleeping-draft.

In ten minutes Una was once more asleep, flinging her subconscious mind across the unthinkable reaches of sheer infinity...

Una's first conception, *via* Olania, was of facing an immense circle of inscrutable, vaguely earthly faces, all at regular distances apart. As she turned slowly on her heels the faces met her in every direction. She was in the center of a colossal room, a solitary and defenceless figure, surveyed by some two hundred of Mars' dignitaries and scientific advisers.

Amongst this circle of erudite creatures there presently rose up the fierce, impetuous figure of Zin himself. He pointed an accusing finger at the silent woman.

"There she stands, a traitor to our cause and our world!" he thundered. "She is the one who planned to travel to earth alone that she might gain the mastery over that planet with her knowledge; she it was who destroyed our beloved Master Laj; she it was who enticed him to the laboratory balcony and then flung him over to his doom. I witnessed it with my own eyes and then brought her here, by force, into the presence of this most Supreme Council of Judicature."

"You bring a grave charge against Olania," commented Ral, Supreme Adjudicator of the Council. "Olania, what have you to say in defence of Zin's statements?"

For a long time the Martian woman remained silent, battling between the ideas of her own mind and those which Una was putting into it. Una won, for a very good reason. For Olania, grief-stricken at Laj's death, was in no condition for exerting her own will to any extent. This alone rendered Una's complicated task easier.

"Zin tells nothing but lies!" Olania burst out at last, passionately. "He himself is the traitor—not me! I will put my cause before you, and pray to the justice of this supreme gathering that I will be heeded. I issue a plea for sentiment—for wise and just thinking. Out of the cosmos, from earth, has come a change of thought—a leaning towards justice. It affected Laj, and it is still affecting me. Laj and I had planned to let earth go free and allow our world to die its natural death. Let our race end for evermore. Zin knows this; he overheard it—then killed Laj to save his own worthless skin. Let him deny it, if he can!"

"A leaning towards sentiment is not for a scientific race," responded Ral with cold decision. "That alone renders you an outcast, Olania. If, of course, Laj *had* ordered our race to cease activity, he would have been incontinently obeyed. As it is, he is dead. And you killed him! You had much in common with Laj, Olania. Only to you did he tell the secret of his two special machines. You had no right to hold that secret from us. What did those machines contain?"

A strange light came into the eyes of Olania at that. She swung round to face Zin.

"Did this devil Zin tell you that?" she demanded fiercely.

"He told us of your confederacy with Laj," Ral conceded gravely. "Quite rightly he believes the machines should be made clear to the Council."

Olania hesitated at that, then a faintly whimsical smile came to her face.

"I gave Laj my solemn word that I would never reveal his secret—but now he is dead I am released from that promise," she said quietly. "The machines are not important, but they are new to our science. Laj knew that with such machines Zin could do many things that would not be for betterment of our race. With those machines, Ral, I can prove my own innocence and Zin's guilt!"

Zin's expression changed. He jumped to his feet again.

"Why are we wasting time discussing these fool machines?" he demanded arrogantly. "We are passing judgment on Olania, not discovering Laj's secrets. Leave that until later."

Ral slowly turned his head to the petulant Martian. "You yourself desired the secret of those machines to be revealed, Zin; your wish shall be gratified," he returned tonelessly. "Proceed, Olania—we will follow."

The girl turned and led the way from the council chamber into Laj's adjoining laboratory. Only once did she pause, and that was to look at the body of the dead ruler, now stretched inert on a nearby table—then, swallowing something in her throat, she moved across to the two machines near the balcony opening, upon which Laj had been secretly engaged.

It was at this point that the mind of Olania overcame that of Una, with the result that the earth-girl was forced to behold purely the actions of Olania herself, swayed by her own mind—and extraordinary actions they presently proved to be, too.

"Proceed," requested Ral's somber voice, and he, Zin, and the Council watched very intently.

Without speaking the girl took several wires that depended from the larger of the two machines, and placed the sucker-like terminals, with which the wires were supplied, on the dead ruler's brow. With the same calmness she switched the machine on, listening for a while to its humming. Then, by means of a hidden lens, there came a white beam of light that presently focussed itself upon a small screen provided for the purpose. The view to Olania—and Una—was familiar.

It represented the Martian woman in every detail, talking quickly but soundlessly, evidently to Laj. For some time this continued, then there appeared the figure of Zin. He mouthed furiously, then became engaged in combat with an invisible foe. The picture reeled crazily, representing what Laj had beheld with his own eyes. It went tumbling down through darkness and finally expired.... Grimly Olania switched the instrument off.

"That is one of Laj's inventions," she explained slowly, her eyes on the glaring Zin. "Capable of reading a dead brain by stimulating the dead cells into momentary life and reproducing by electric currents the exact things last witnessed by the optic nerves. Laj knew what use Zin could make of such an instrument—that was why he refrained from explaining it. He knew Zin to be a traitor and an assassin. Can there be any more doubt in your mind, Ral, that Zin is the culprit?"

All eyes turned to the villainous Martian.

Quite abruptly, however, he turned swiftly, started to run, and before a single hand could be raised to stop him he had vaulted the balcony rail and dropped out into the blackness beyond.

Followed a long silence.

"Olania, you have proved yourself guiltless," Ral murmured, placing his arm round the woman's massive shoulders. "But we still have no proof that Laj ever said our race should die and leave earth unmolested."

"That brings me to Laj's second and last secret invention," she answered quietly. "You will know, of course, that sound-waves travel outwards until they are imprisoned by the higher reaches of the atmosphere?"

Ral nodded, and the girl turned to the second machine.

"Here again Zin could have learned many secrets that were not intended for his prying ears. Hence Laj's caution. Now listen…"

Olania set to work with the various dials and operated the complicated sound-detecting mechanisms. For a long time a weird medley of unwanted sounds came surging through, and then unwanted voices; at last, as the Council was getting impatient, came the right sequence.

"It is better that we admit our progress has ended— that our race has run its course and must die there. Progress further we cannot; we can only live in what we have already attained— So be it, then. I, the King-Lord, have proclaimed it. Our world shall die! Earth shall be freed! Tomorrow, I will inform our peoples; they cannot defy my edict. Tonight I will stop the etheric barrier machine and remove the danger to earth's peoples. After that— comes the end…"

And so, gradually, the machine went on, giving verbatim everything that had been spoken, even through Zin's fierce words and altercation, as further proof of his unquestionable guilt. When it was over Ral raised his hand.

"It is enough," he said steadily, bowing his head. "The King-Lord ordained it; it is for us to obey." He turned to the members of the Council grouped about him. "Give the order at once for the stoppage of the etheric barrier machine—stop the Brain Controllers—stop all machines likely to endanger earth... He paused and turned to the now silent girl.

"And you, Olania?" he enquired gently. "You admit that you loved Laj? You said you did. He spoke of some extramundane matehood, too highly elevated for our minds to grasp..."

The Martian woman nodded slowly. "I am the master of my death, as I have been of my life, Ral," she replied quietly. "Leave me alone for a moment, please. I have here a tiny capsule"—she held out her hand—"which by an instant's pressure will release through a self-inflicted cut in my hand a poison, into my blood-stream, bringing instant death. I am dying sooner than you others—that is all."

"You have courage, Olania," Ral commented thoughtfully.

"To meet death does not require courage; to meet *life* it is that requires it," came the strange reply, and with that Olania walked across to where the dead Laj lay upon the table. Without hesitation she climbed up and lay down beside him. Her right hand closed tightly; came a faint crackling sound as the capsule broke...

With slow dignity Ral went over to her, stood for some time looking down at her limply dangling hand, blood clotting the palm—then his gaze moved to her peaceful, faintly smiling face and closed eyes.

Ral raised his hand in silent salutation.

"So be it," he murmured. "Our race has run its course; it is the end." Then blackness descended…

* * * *

Una came slowly to her senses in the armchair to find three worried faces surveying her. Stimulants brought a rapid return of her faculties, and at length she was able to answer the myriad questions that were hurled at her. Quietly she answered them all.

"So, partly influenced by my mind, and partly by her own, Olania saved the earth," she concluded at last. "When she killed herself at the finish I was permitted to still see the man, Ral, for a short period, presumably because the brain did not die on the instant. My last vision was his salutation. That broke the subconscious union for ever. Man and woman will be unhampered ever after this."

And such indeed proved to be correct. From that moment onwards nobody on earth ever dreamed; people who formerly had possessed mediumistic and clairvoyant tendencies were suddenly devoid of them—all strange inexplicable conditions of the brain vanished completely and absolutely. Yet progress went on, mainly because, even as Moore had once theorized, man could not unlearn knowledge. So the result was a happier earth, and a much less mentally terrorized peoples,

But only a Surrey schoolmaster, who later ascended to a headship and a comfortable salary, and his practical, unselfish wife knew the reason why. Dr. Mason had died fairly early in life, and Sir Arthur had destroyed himself in an accidental explosion, so only Mr. and Mrs. Moore Holmes possessed the secret.

In all the world only they knew that the answer lay in a red planet, which they often viewed across the south country meadows—a planet wherein lay a dead race, the secret of subconscious control sealed for ever in brains and bodies that were frozen into the relentless coldness of infinity itself...

ABOUT THE AUTHOR

British writer **JOHN RUSSELL FEARN** was born near Manchester, England, in 1908. As a child he devoured the science fiction of Wells and Verne, and was a voracious reader of the Boys' Story Papers. He was also fascinated by the cinema, and first broke into print in 1931 with a series of articles in *Film Weekly*.

He then quickly sold his first novel, *The Intelligence Gigantic*, to the American magazine, *Amazing Stories*. Over the next fifteen years, writing under several pseudonyms, Fearn became one of the most prolific contributors to all of the leading US science fiction pulps, including such legendary publications as *Astounding Stories*, *Startling Stories*, *Thrilling Wonder Stories*, and *Weird Tales*.

During the late 1940s he diversified into writing novels for the UK market, and also created his famous super-woman character, The Golden Amazon, for the prestigious Canadian magazine, the Toronto *Star Weekly*. In the early 1950s in the UK, his fifty-two novels as "Vargo Statten" were bestsellers, most notably his novelization of the film, *Creature from the Black Lagoon*.

Apart from science fiction, he had equal success with westerns, romances, and detective fiction, writing an amazing total of 180 novels—most of them in a period of just ten years—before his early death in 1960. His work has been translated into nine languages, and continues to be reprinted and read worldwide.

The G-Bomb: A Science Fiction Novel
Here and Now: A Science Fiction Novel
Into the Unknown: A Science Fiction Tale
Last Conflict: Classic Science Fiction Stories
Legacy from Sirius: A Classic Science Fiction Novel
The Man from Hell: Classic Science Fiction Stories
The Man Who Was Not: A Crime Novel
Manton's World: A Classic Science Fiction Novel
Moon Magic: A Novel of Romance (as Elizabeth Rutland)
One Way Out: A Crime Novel (with Philip Harbottle)
Pattern of Murder: A Classic Crime Novel
Reflected Glory: A Dr. Castle Classic Crime Novel
*Robbery Without Violence: Two Science Fiction Crime
    Stories*
Rule of the Brains: Classic Science Fiction Stories
Shattering Glass: A Crime Novel
The Silvered Cage: A Scientific Murder Mystery
Slaves of Ijax: A Science Fiction Novel
Something from Mercury: Classic Science Fiction Stories
The Space Warp: A Science Fiction Novel
The Time Trap: A Science Fiction Novel
Valley of Pretenders: Classic Science Fiction Stories
Vision Sinister: A Scientific Detective Thriller
Voice of the Conqueror: A Classic Science Fiction Novel
What Happened to Hammond? A Scientific Mystery
Within That Room!: A Classic Crime Novel
World Without Chance: Classic Science Fiction Stories

www.ingramcontent.com/pod-product-compliance
Lightning Source LLC
Chambersburg PA
CBHW050757250626
47155CB00005B/2112